Lucy Monroe

—

An Heiress for His Empire

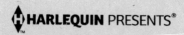
HARLEQUIN PRESENTS®

Recycling programs
for this product may
not exist in your area.

ISBN-13: 978-0-373-13757-2

AN HEIRESS FOR HIS EMPIRE

First North American Publication 2014

For questions and comments about the quality of this book, please contact us at CustomerService@Harlequin.com.

Printed in U.S.A.

HARLEQUIN®
www.Harlequin.com

Viktor's kiss took Maddie by surprise. It shouldn't have. Wasn't it natural to kiss to seal an engagement?

But the kiss did surprise her. And then it overwhelmed her, his lips coaxing a response that radiated throughout her body. They took possession of hers, insisting on the two things she'd said only that morning she wasn't capable of.

Submission and trust.

But then, like with so many other things in her life, the rules did not apply to Viktor Beck.

She found herself melting into him, no thoughts for self-preservation or holding anything back.

And he accepted her surrender with a forceful masculine desire that belied any claim for a lack of passion between them.

He devoured her mouth, his arms coming around her, his hands pressing her body flush with his.

Maddie's knees would have given out but Vik's hold on her was too tight.

The kiss was Viktor Beck staking claim to the woman who promised to marry him and give him his dreams.

Lucy Monroe's

Ruthless Russians

Passion is in their blood

As boys, they came from Russia to America to make their fortunes. Now formidable opponents in the boardroom, Viktor Beck and Maxwell Black are about to make the biggest acquisitions of their lives by marrying two of San Francisco's most notorious heiresses! Beneath their suave American exteriors beat the passionate hearts of fearsome Cossack warriors—and their intended brides are about to give them the battle of their lives!

An Heiress for His Empire

A tabloid sex scandal means Viktor Beck can put his plan in motion and marry heiress Madison Archer— the key to taking over her father's business and building his empire. But even this ruthless Russian is not prepared for his wild bride to be a virgin!

October 2014

A Virgin for His Prize

Formidable CEO Maxwell Black is about to make his ultimate acquisition—socialite Romi Grayson! She has something he wants, and his need for control— in all areas—means he won't rest until his ring is on her finger...and the innocent Romi is warm and willing in his bed!

November 2014

All about the author...
Lucy Monroe

Award-winning and bestselling author **LUCY MONROE** sold her first book in September of 2002 to the Harlequin Presents® line. That book represented a dream that had been burning in her heart for years—the dream to share her stories with readers who love romance as much as she does. Since then she has sold more than thirty books to three publishers and hit national bestseller lists in the U.S. and England, but what has touched her most deeply since selling that first book are the reader letters she receives. Her most important goal with every book is to touch a reader's heart, and when she hears she's done that, it makes every night spent writing into the wee hours of morning worth it.

She started reading Harlequin Presents® books very young and discovered a heroic type of man between the covers of those books...an honorable man, capable of faithfulness and sacrifice for the people he loves. Now married to what she terms her "alpha male at the end of a book," Lucy believes there is a lot more reality to the fantasy stories she writes than most people give credit for. She believes in happy endings that are really marvelous beginnings, and that's why she writes them. She hopes her books help readers to believe a little, too... just as romance did for her so many years ago.

She really does love to hear from readers and responds to every email. You can reach her by emailing lucymonroe@lucymonroe.com.

Other titles by Lucy Monroe available in ebook:

SHEIKH'S SCANDAL *(The Chatsfield)*
MILLION DOLLAR CHRISTMAS PROPOSAL
PRINCE OF SECRETS *(By His Royal Decree)*
ONE NIGHT HEIR *(By His Royal Decree)*

For Judy Flohr, a very special reader who I have long considered an honest friend. It's sort of amazing to me that you've been reading and sharing your love of my books since the very first one, *The Greek Tycoon's Ultimatum* back in 2003. When I'm doubting myself or the story, I know I can reread your emails or online reader reviews and remember why I write and that maybe I'm not so bad at this after all.

THANK YOU! Hugs and blessings, Lucy

CHAPTER ONE

MADISON ARCHER SET her morning coffee down, hot liquid spilling over the rim, as she read her Google alerts with growing horror.

Madcap Madison Looking for New Master?
Archer Heiress into Heavy Kink
San Francisco Bad Boy Dumps Very Bad Girl

The articles made lurid claims about a lifestyle and relationship between Maddie and Perry Timwater. A completely nonexistent relationship.

The fact that Perry was the source caused the coffee to sour in Maddie's stomach.

His supposed exposé of their fictitious relationship claimed she was a submissive with a serious pain fetish and need for multiple partners. She gritted her teeth on the urge to swear as she read it was her inability to remain faithful that forced Perry to end things between them.

Maddie wouldn't mind ending Perry right that minute. Betrayal choked her.

How could he have done this?

He was her *friend*.

They'd met their freshman year at university. He'd made her laugh when she'd thought nothing could. Not after her epic fail trying to get Viktor Beck's attention. She'd started university with a broken heart and Perry had helped her paste over the cracks with friendship.

She'd helped him pass his accountancy courses. He'd played platonic escort for her and she'd provided him entrée to Jeremy Archer's world—an echelon above his own.

But never, not once, had their friendship ever taken a turn toward something heavier.

Pounding sounded on her front door. "Maddie! It's me, don't freak." Then barely a second later, the double snick of locks sliding back was followed by the door swinging wide.

Holding a bag from their favorite bakery aloft, her black bob swirling around her pixie face, Romi Grayson kicked the door shut behind her. "I come bearing the panacea for all ills."

"I'm not sure even chocolate and flaky pastry can make this situation better." Maddie slumped against the back of her chair.

Eyes the same vibrant blue as Maddie's glittered with anger. "So, Perry's lost his mind, right?"

"You saw the articles?"

"Only after reporters woke me from a dead sleep demanding my opinion of my best friend's darker sexual proclivities." Romi's mouth twisted wryly. "Proclivities I'm pretty sure you wouldn't have even if you *weren't* still a virgin."

"You've got that right. I've never been able to trust one man enough to have sex, much less multiple partners."

As ridiculous as that might seem at twenty-four, it wasn't going to change anytime soon, either.

"If you ask me, it's got less to do with trust and more to do with the fact you imprinted on Viktor Beck like a baby bird when you were a teenager and you've never gotten over him."

"Romi!" Maddie was in no mood to hash out her unrequited feelings for her father's dark-haired, dark-eyed, to-die-for-bodied golden boy.

"I'm just saying…"

"Nothing you haven't said before." Maddie's stomach grew queasier by the second.

Along with the rest of the world, Vik would see the articles, but she couldn't afford to think about that right now, or she really was going to lose it. "Father is going to kill me."

This new scandal was bound to crack even the

San Francisco tycoon's icy demeanor. And not in the way Maddie had always craved.

He'd sent her away to boarding school months after her mother's death and Maddie had courted media attention in the hopes of gaining his. It had worked for her mother, Helene Archer, née Madison, the original Madcap Madison, but Maddie had come to realize the strategy had backfired pretty spectacularly for her.

In the nine years since Helene's death, Jeremy had developed a habit of thinking the worst of his daughter. When he wasn't ignoring her existence all together.

"If he doesn't die of a stress-related heart attack first." Romi put a chocolate-filled croissant in front of Maddie.

"Don't say that."

The other woman grimaced. "Sorry. Stuff just comes out. You know what I'm like. Your dad is wound pretty tight, though."

Maddie couldn't argue that.

"I think this time, Perry's diarrhea of the mouth has me beat anyway." Romi chewed her pastry militantly. "What was he thinking?"

Morose, Maddie stared at her friend. "That he wanted the money the tabloid paid him for the story?"

She'd had no idea that turning down his latest request for a loan would result in her utter humiliation. How could she? Friends didn't do that to each other.

"Jerk."

Maddie usually played peacemaker between her two closest friends, but she wasn't about to stand up for Perry this time. "What am I going to do?"

"You could threaten to sue and demand a retraction."

"Based on my word against his?"

Romi made a sound very close to a growl. "You two have never even kissed with tongue."

"But we have kissed, for the cameras." Perry had always made a joke of it.

He had been Maddie's go-to escort for years and more than one article speculating on their relationship had been run, often quoting anonymous sources and always accompanied by the joke kissing pictures.

"Do you think he's done this before?"

"Sold *confidential details* of your supposed relationship?" Romi asked.

"Yes."

"You know what I think."

Maddie sighed. "That he's a leech."

"Always has been."

"He was a good friend." Maddie couldn't make herself claim he *still* was.

Romi just gave Maddie a disbelieving look, no words necessary.

Ignoring it, Maddie said, "I probably can't prove we never had a relationship, but I can sue them for libel in the details."

"His word against yours."

"But he's lying."

"This is something new for the tabloids?"

Feeling hopeless, Maddie pushed her croissant away.

"You could always sic your dad's dogs on Perry. That media fixer of his could be cast in Shark Week on the Discovery Channel."

"I should." Even supposing her dad cared enough to assign his media fixer's precious time to helping Maddie.

Romi's expression turned knowing. "But you won't. Perry was your friend."

Maddie opened her mouth, but Romi put her hand up, forestalling words. "Don't you dare say he still is."

"No." Maddie swallowed back emotion. "No, it's pretty clear he's not my friend and maybe he never was."

"Oh, sweetie." Romi came around the table to hug her.

Maddie fought down stress-induced nausea. "I thought he was real."

"Instead, he turned out to be just another one

of the plastic people." Romi's tone reflected her own experience with that. "All looks and no substance."

Maddie choked out a morbid laugh. "Yeah."

A bugler's reveille sounded from her smartphone.

With a snicker, Romi moved back to her seat. "Daddy's PA?"

"I thought it was appropriate." Maddie clicked into her text messages, unsurprised to see that there were dozens.

While she checked her phone periodically throughout the day, Maddie only had sound alerts set for certain people: Romi, Perry—who was going off the list today—Maddie's father, his personal assistant. Viktor Beck.

Not that her father's business heir apparent contacted Maddie these days. But still, if he did…she'd get an audible alert.

Ignoring the numerous messages from *friends*, acquaintances and the media jackals, Maddie clicked into the one from her father's PA.

Mtg w Mr. Archer @ 10:45—conf rm 2.

Mr. Archer. Not Mr. A, even though the PA had used text speak for the rest of the message. Not *your father*. That might have been too personal.

"He wants to meet this morning." Maddie bit

her lip, considering what she'd have to change to make that happen.

Romi nodded. "Are you going to go?"

Maddie considered putting off her morning plans for the meeting with her father.

"No." It wasn't as if her showing up when he called was going to make Jeremy any less angry.

She shot a quick text back to the PA offering to come anytime after noon-thirty.

Fifteen minutes later, Romi was gone after a final pep talk when the strains of Michael Bublé's "Call Me Irresponsible" sounded from Maddie's smartphone.

Her father was *calling* her. Personally. Not texting.

Any other time, she would be thrilled. But right now? The crooner's smooth voice was as ominous as the sepulchre tones of a Halloween horror flick's sound track.

Maddie put the phone to her ear. "Hello, Father."

"Ten forty-five, Madison. You will not be late."

"You know I have a standing morning appointment." Not that he knew what it was.

Maddie had tried to tell him once, but Jeremy had mocked the very idea of his flighty daughter doing anything worthwhile. Worse, he'd made it clear how useless he thought it was to spend time volunteering at an underfunded public school predominantly populated by the children of poverty-level families.

Since then, Maddie had kept her two lives completely separate. Maddie Grace, nondescript twentysomething who loved children and volunteered a good chunk of her time, had nothing in common—not even hair and eye color—with Madison Archer, notorious socialite and heiress.

"Cancel." No give. No explanation. Just demand.

Typical.

"It's important."

"No. It is not." His tone was so cold it sent shivers along her extremities.

"It is to me." She wished she could be as unaffected by his displeasure as he was by hers. "Please."

"Ten-forty-five, Madison." Then he hung up. She knew because the call dropped.

Wearing the armor of her socialite Madison Archer persona, Maddie got off the elevator at the twenty-ninth floor of her father's building in San Francisco's financial district.

None of the nerves wreaking havoc with her insides showed on her smooth face.

Makeup applied to highlight, not compete with, the blue of her eyes and gentle bow of her lips, she'd styled her chin-length red hair in perfectly placed curls around her oval face so like her mother's. No highlights had ever been necessary for the natural copper tones.

Her three-quarter-length-sleeved Valentino black-and-white suit wasn't this year's collection, but it was one of her favorites and fit the image she intended to convey. The wide black banded hem of the straight skirt brushed a proper two inches above her knees and the Jackie-O-style jacket with a statement bow was a galaxy away from slutty.

She'd opted for classic closed-toe black Jimmy Choo pumps that added a mere two inches to her five-foot-six-inch height. Maddie carried a simple leather Chanel bag, her accessories limited to her mother's favorite Cartier watch and diamond stud earrings.

Maddie didn't look anything like the woman described by Perry in his "breakup interview" with the press.

She walked into Conference Room Two without knocking, stopping for a strategic pause in the doorway to allow the other occupants a moment to look their fill.

She wasn't going to scurry in like a mouse trying to avoid the cat's attention.

The brief moment had the added benefit of allowing her to take her own *lay of the land*.

Seven people sat around the eight-person conference table. As to be expected, her father occupied one end. Maddie was equal parts relieved and worried to see his media fixer at the other end, but not happy at all to see the man seated to the right of her father.

Romi was right that Maddie had had a crush on the gorgeous Viktor Beck since he started working for Jeremy Archer ten years ago. The unrequited feelings had evolved from schoolgirl infatuation to something more, something that made it impossible for other men to measure up.

That first year, Maddie had still had her mother and Helene would tease Maddie for her blushes in the tycoon-in-the-making's presence.

Maddie had learned to control her blushes, but not the feelings the handsome third-generation Russian engendered in her.

Having him here to witness her humiliation tightened the knot of tension inside her until she wasn't sure it would ever come undone.

Less understandable, but not nearly as upsetting, was the presence of two of her father's other high-level managers in the remaining chairs on that side of the table. Her father's PA sat to his left, with an empty chair beside her.

The final man at the table had a powerful presence and a familiar face, but in her current state of highly guarded stress, Maddie couldn't place him.

Everyone had a stack of papers in front of them. It took only the briefest glance to see what they were: printed-out copies of the news stories Maddie had seen earlier on her smartphone. Underneath them was an individual copy for each person in the room of the actual tabloid the original story had run in.

Vik's pile was different. It had what looked like a contract on top. Looking around the table, Maddie realized everyone else had a copy of that as well, but on the bottom of their pile—the stapled corner was the only thing visible in the other piles.

She looked at her father and gave him the sardonic expression she'd been using for years to mask her vulnerability. "I don't suppose it occurred to you to discuss this with me privately before bringing in a think tank."

"Sit down, Madison." He didn't even bother to respond to her comment.

Which should neither surprise, nor hurt. So why did it do both?

She waited a count of three before obeying his brusque order, deliberately ignoring the stack of papers in front of her. "I assume we've already drafted a letter demanding a retraction?"

When her father didn't answer, she stared pointedly at his media fixer.

"Is it likely your ex-lover will recant his commentary?" the fixer asked in a flat tone.

"First, he was never my lover. Second, he doesn't have to recant his lies for us to sue the tabloid for libel." Though her chances of winning the suit weren't high without Perry's honesty.

"I am not in the habit of wasting time or resources on a hopeless endeavor," her father said.

"The story is out there and that can't be changed," she agreed. "But that doesn't mean we leave Perry's lies unchallenged."

Her father's eyes were chips of blue ice. "If you wish to challenge your ex-lover's *lies*, you may do so, but that is not my concern."

"You don't believe the stories?" she asked with a pained incredulity she couldn't quite hide.

"What I believe is not the issue at hand."

"It is for me." There were only two people in that room whose opinion Maddie cared about.

Her father's and Viktor Beck's, no matter how much she might wish that wasn't the case.

Her gaze shifted to Vik, but nothing from the stern set of his square jaw to the obscure depths of his espresso-brown eyes revealed his thoughts.

There had been a time when he might have tried to encourage her with a half smile or even a wink, but those days were gone. There'd been no softening in his demeanor toward her since her first trip home after going away to university.

And while that might be her own fault, she didn't have to like it.

Her father cleared his throat. "Those tawdry stories may have precipitated this meeting, but they are not the reason for it."

Maddie's attention snapped back to her only remaining family. "What do you mean?"

"The issue we are here to address is your unacceptable notoriety, Madison. I will not sit by while you attempt to rival other heiresses for worldwide infamy."

"I don't." Even when Maddie had tried to court her father's attention by gaining that of the media, she hadn't gone that far.

Okay, so she and Romi were known for their participation in political rallies of the liberal variety, which included a well-publicized sit-in protesting cuts in local school funding. That Maddie had gone further, bungee jumping from the Golden Gate Bridge with five others and unfurling a giant banner that read Go Green or Go Home, was beside the point.

There were videos online of her bungee jumping in less politically motivated and slightly more risky circumstances. The snowboarding had been a total failure, but she'd always loved downhill skiing and learning to jump had been fantastic. Of course, only her tumbles made it into the media.

But she hadn't done a thing to get herself in the papers in over six months. Not since hitting the headlines with a nighttime adventure in skydiving that had resulted in her hospitalization with a hairline fracture to her pelvis.

Her father had not only ignored her exploit, but he'd also ignored Maddie's injury. And not only had he refused to take her phone calls from the hospital, but he'd also made it clear, through his PA, that Maddie was not welcome at the family mansion for her recovery.

She'd been forced to hire a nurse to help during the weeks of her limited mobility. Romi had offered to stay with her, but Maddie refused to take advantage.

"Am I to understand you didn't read Madison in on the contents of this contract?" Vik asked, unexpected disapproval edging his deep tone. "Do you actually expect her to agree?"

"She'll agree." Her father gave her a stern glare. "Or I will cut her out of my life completely."

The words were painful enough to hear, but the absolute conviction in her father's voice stabbed straight through Maddie's carefully cultivated facade to the genuine and all-too-vulnerable emotions underneath.

"Over this?" she demanded, waving her hand toward the printed articles. "It's not true!"

"You will not continue to drag my name and that of my company through the mud, Madison."

"I don't *do* that." While she'd managed a certain level of media notoriety, it had never before been because of anything even remotely like the lies Perry had spewed to the tabloids.

Her father began reading the headlines out loud and weak tears burned the back of her eyes. Maddie refused to give in to them, wishing she could be as genuinely emotionless as the steel-gray-haired man flaying her with other people's words.

"I told you, *he lied.*"

"Why would he?" the media fixer asked, sounding interested in an almost clinical way.

"For money. For revenge." Because she'd turned him down one too many times and compounded that by refusing his latest request for a loan. "I don't know, but he lied."

How many times did she have to say it?

"It is time for definitive measures to be taken," Jeremy said, as if she hadn't spoken.

"On that at least, we can agree, beginning with the demand for a retraction. I can do my own interview." Even though she hated that kind of direct contact with the media.

She considered offering the ultimate sacrifice of integrating her Maddie Grace life with that of socialite Madison Archer in order to combat the negative image that clearly concerned her father.

Jeremy dismissed her offer with a slicing gesture. "I believe I've made it clear that the current scandal is not my primary concern."

"What is your concern?" she asked, confused.

"The capricious lifestyle that has resulted in your unacceptable and notorious reputation."

"You want me to come work for AIH?" she asked with zero enthusiasm and even less belief.

The last time the issue of Archer International Holdings had come up, her father had made it clear he no longer harbored dreams of her one day taking over.

His harsh bark of laughter was all the answer she needed. "Absolutely not."

"You want me to get a job somewhere else?" She could do that.

She preferred using her education as a volunteer teacher's aide, but if it would help her relationship with her father, she would get a paying job—which hopefully wouldn't conflict with her volunteering schedule.

More derisive laughter fell from her father's lips. "Do you really think any reputable charity or business would hire you right now?"

Heat climbed up her neck, ending in a very rare blush. She'd become adept at hiding her emotions, even suppressing her blushes of embarrassment a long time ago.

But suddenly, she realized that if it *did* become known that Madison Archer was Maddie Grace, the school might be forced to disallow Maddie's volunteering. All because a man she'd thought was a friend had turned out to be a lying, manipulative, opportunistic user.

"He wants you to get married," Vik informed her, no indication in his tone or demeanor that he was joking.

Her father did not jump in with a denial, either.

For the first time, she looked around the room to see how the other occupants were reacting. Her father's media fixer and PA were both busy on their tablets, ignoring the conversation now, or giving a pretty good pretense of doing so.

One of his managers was looking at her with the type of speculation that left Madison feeling dirty, but the fact he had the articles about her spread out in front of him could have something to do with that, too.

The other manager was reading through the paperwork and the man who Maddie did not know was looking at her father, his expression assessing.

Vik's expression was enigmatic as always.

She met her father's gaze again, finding nothing there but implacable resolve. "You want me to get married."

"Yes."

"Who?" she asked, unhappily certain she already had an inkling.

"One of these four men." Her father indicated Vik, the two other managers and the man she did not know. "You know Viktor, of course, and I am sure you remember Steven Whitley." Jeremy nodded toward a manager she was fairly certain had been divorced once already and was nearly twice her age.

Maddie found herself acknowledging both men with a tip of her own head in some bizarre ritual of polite behavior. Or maybe it was just the situation that was so bizarre.

He indicated the manager whose look had given her the willies. "Brian Jones."

His expression was benign now, almost pitying.

"I thought you were engaged," she said, her voice almost as tight as her throat. But that couldn't be helped.

Hadn't Maddie met his fiancée at the last Christmas party?

"Are you?" her father asked, annoyance clear in his tone. "Miss Priest?"

His PA looked up from her tablet with a frown. "Yes, sir?"

"Jones is engaged."

"Is he?" Miss Priest didn't sound concerned. "He is not married."

"But I will be." Brian stood. "I don't believe I'll be needed for the rest of this meeting, if you'll excuse me, sir?"

"Did you read the contract?" her father demanded.

"I did."

"And you are still leaving?"

"Yes, sir."

A measure of respect shone in her father's eyes even as he frowned. "Then go." He nodded toward the stranger on the other side of Maddie as if the introductions had not been interrupted by the defection of one of his candidates. "Maxwell Black, CEO of BIT."

Maxwell smiled at her, magnetism that might actually rival Vik's exuding from him. "Hello, Madison. It's good to see you again."

He wasn't overtly sexual, but there was a vibe to him that made Maddie wrap her arms protectively around herself. This man carried power around him the same way Vik did, but with a predatory edge she hadn't experienced from her father's heir apparent.

Then, she'd never been his business rival.

"I don't believe we've met?" She forced her arms to fall to her sides.

"I saw you at the Red Ball last February."

She remembered going to the charity event that raised money for research into heart disease, but she didn't remember seeing him.

"I would have remembered."

"I'm glad to hear you say so." His teeth flashed

in a blinding white smile. "But I meant what I said. I saw you there. We were not introduced."

"Oh."

Her father cleared his throat in that disapproving way he had, but if he expected Maddie to say it was a pleasure to meet the man—under these circumstances—he didn't know her very well.

But then that had been her problem most of her life, hadn't it?

CHAPTER TWO

THE MORNING HAD gone according to Viktor's plans so far, but the spark of temper in Madison's brilliant blue eyes threatened to derail it.

If Jeremy had evinced even one iota of the concern Viktor knew the older man felt for his daughter's current predicament, she would be reacting very differently. But then if father and daughter got along perfectly, or even very well, Viktor's own plans would by necessity be very different.

"You know, I never even entertained the fantasy that you called me to help me, to take *my side* for once, to protect me because I mattered to you." The beautiful redhead offered the emotionally laden words in a flat tone Viktor almost envied.

She would be one hell of a poker player.

She was lying, though. Madison wouldn't have shown up if she didn't think her father would help her.

"You never were a child taken with fairy tales," Jeremy said.

Viktor could have reined in the older man's prideful idiocy, but that wouldn't further his own agenda. However, he felt an unexpected pang of guilt at Madison's barely there flinch and flash of pain in the azure depths of her eyes.

She recovered quickly, her expression smooth—almost bored. "No, that was always Mom's department. She lived under the fallacy that you cared about us. I know better."

It was Jeremy's turn to flinch and he wasn't as fast at hiding his reaction as his daughter, but then he had to be in shock. Madison didn't go for the jugular like that. In fact, in all the arguments between the tycoon and his daughter Viktor had been privy to, he'd never heard Madison use her mother's memory against her father before.

No triumph at the emotional bloodletting showed on Madison's porcelain features.

Instead, she looked like she wanted nothing more than to get up and walk away. The fact she stayed in her seat was proof the heiress might be criminally flagrant in her personal life, but she wasn't stupid.

She knew her father well enough to be aware that Jeremy's arsenal of threats wasn't empty.

"You have five minutes." Madison's words verified she did indeed realize her father had more *encouragement* to lay on the table, but also that she had little patience in waiting to find out what it was.

Color washed over Jeremy's face. "Excuse me?"

"She wants the other two prongs to the pitchfork," Viktor informed his boss.

Jeremy's scowl said he knew that's what she'd meant, but he didn't like the time limit or implied ultimatum that Madison would get up and leave if it wasn't met.

"Pitchfork?" Black asked.

Viktor could have answered, but he didn't. Giving Maxwell Black any kind of information wasn't on his agenda for the day. Viktor had ignored the presence of the other *candidates* at the table as superfluous, and planned to continue to do so.

Madison wasn't so reticent. "Jeremy never enters a fight he isn't sure he can win. To that end, he stacks the deck. He'll have three scenarios in the offing, none of which will I want to eventuate."

"You call your father by his first name?" Black asked.

Madison flicked a meaning-laden glance in the tycoon's direction. "As he pointed out, I'm the not the one in the family to wallow in sentimental fantasy."

What she didn't say was that until that morning,

Madison had called Jeremy Archer *Father* and sometimes even *Dad*. That she would no longer do so could be taken from her words as a given.

No question that the company president had seriously messed up in his approach to his daughter.

Viktor might have suggested the current course to protect AIH's interests and future, but he would not have blindsided Madison with it during a meeting with strangers.

He'd been angry when he realized Jeremy hadn't even bothered to brief his daughter about the meeting's agenda before her arrival. She might be flighty and prone to inauspicious, risky behavior, but she deserved more respect than that.

Viktor had no doubts that Jeremy would ultimately get what he wanted, not least of which because Viktor would make it happen.

However he had a nascent suspicion that the personal cost for that success might be higher for Jeremy than the president of Archer International Holdings anticipated.

Madison flicked a glance at the Cartier watch on her wrist. "Your time starts now, Jeremy."

"Golden Chances Charter School."

"What about it?" Madison asked with caution, the barest crack in her calm facade finally showing.

"Over the last three years, you have donated tens of thousands of dollars from your Madison Trust income to school improvements and projects."

"I am aware."

But Viktor hadn't been. He began to wonder what else he didn't know about Madison.

Jeremy's eyes, the only feature truly like his daughter's, reflected subtle triumph. "The school's zoning is under scrutiny."

"It wasn't as of yesterday."

"Things change."

"I see." Madison glanced pointedly down at her watch.

"Are you pretending that does not matter to you?"

"No. You have two more minutes."

Viktor was impressed. Madison would have done a better job negotiating a recent deal with a Japanese conglomerate than the project manager they'd sent to Asia.

Jeremy frowned. "Ramona Grayson."

"What about her?"

Viktor would be crossing his legs protectively if that tone and look had been directed at him.

"Her father is a drunk," Jeremy pointed out with well-known derision toward a man Madison had made no bones about considering a second father.

"And mine is a conscienceless bastard. I guess we both lost in the masculine parent lottery, though given a choice I'd pick Harry Grayson. His emotions might be pickled with alcohol, but at least he has them."

Viktor had seen Madison angry. He'd seen her hurt, embarrassed and even seriously disappointed. He had never seen her this coldly furious.

The Madison that Viktor had known for ten years was in no way reflected in the harshly dismissive woman in front of them.

Despite the implication of her words, she loved her father. In the past, she hadn't been able to hide her need for his attention and approval. Her mistake had always been how she went about getting it.

She'd followed in her mother's footsteps, not realizing Jeremy Archer had been too traumatized by the loss of his wife to want to see her audacious nature reflected in their only child.

"Do you think Ramona sees it that way?" Jeremy asked. "Or perhaps she would prefer a father not lost in a bottle."

Madison shrugged. "It's not something we discuss."

"Nevertheless, the destruction of her father's business, followed by him losing everything to bankruptcy, would hurt her a great deal. Don't you think?"

Madison pulled her phone from her purse with an almost negligent move belied by the blue fire in her gaze. "You have exactly fifteen seconds to take that tactic for coercion off the table."

"Or what?"

"Ten."

And for the first time in Viktor's memory, infallible businessman Jeremy Archer made a mistake in negotiating. He silently called his daughter's bluff.

He believed that because she had no interest in business, Madison was not capable of the same level of ruthlessness as he was.

Viktor knew from personal experience that just because a parent and child lived very different lives, it did not mean that they shared no common personality traits.

Madison pressed her phone to her ear.

"Don't," Viktor said.

Madison just shook her head. "I'm sorry, Viktor."

There would be only one reason for her to apologize to him. Whatever she had planned would have a detrimental effect on AIH and, by default, Viktor's job and livelihood.

The possible implications were still firming in his brain as she made contact with the lawyer in charge of the Madison Trust. "Hello, Mr.

Bellingham. I need you to draw some papers up for me. I'm texting you the instructions now."

Seconds later the lawyer's agitated tones came through her phone.

Madison listened for a moment in silence and then replied. "Yes, he knows. He's sitting right here. In fact, he's the one who put this in motion."

The fact the unflappable Bellingham was still speaking loudly enough for Viktor to almost make out his words said something about the nature of Madison's instructions.

"I am absolutely certain, and Mr. Bellingham? If your firm wishes to keep the Madison Trust as a client in sixty-five days when it falls under my control, I suggest you have those papers ready for me to sign when I stop by your office later this afternoon."

Another spate of conversation, this time quieter. "Thank you, Mr. Bellingham."

Madison tucked her phone back into her purse and faced her father, her expression daring him to ask what she'd done.

Jeremy remained stubbornly silent, or maybe he was in too much shock to react. He had to realize the likely content of those papers, or maybe he didn't.

Maybe Jeremy Archer was under the mistaken impression that Archer International Holdings was important enough to his daughter that she would not do what Viktor was almost positive she had done.

"What do the papers say?" Viktor asked, unwilling to make decisions based on assumptions.

"As you know, because of the financial deal Grandfather Madison made with Jeremy upon his marriage to my mother, the Madison Trust holds twenty-five percent of the privately held shares in Archer International Holdings."

"Those shares are your heritage," Jeremy said.

"Romi is my friend."

"So you gave her some of your shares?" Viktor asked with no real hope it could be that simple.

"If Mr. Grayson's company is under threat from AIH or any company remotely affiliated with it, at one minute past midnight on my twenty-fifth birthday, all of those shares will be signed over to Harry Grayson personally. Not his company."

"You cannot do that!"

"I can." Madison looked more like her father in that moment than at any other time Viktor had known her.

"And if his company is not under threat?" Viktor asked, suspecting that Jeremy's calling his daughter's threat had precipitated some kind of permanent action on her part.

"Half of my shares will be signed over to Romi."

Jeremy stood up, his face flushing with color, his eyes narrowed in fury. "You will not sign those papers."

"I will." Conversely, Madison relaxed back into her chair. "You had your chance to take my friend's happiness off the table as a negotiating point, but you refused to take it."

"That's insane," Steven Whitley said, speaking up for the first time since his introduction to Madison. "Even half of your shares are valued at tens of millions."

"Romi won't have to worry about her drunk of a father ruining *her* life, will she?" Madison asked her father, as if he'd been the one to bring up the point of the shares' value.

Jeremy slammed his hand on the table. "I am not ruining your life, Madison, you've done a fair job of that yourself."

"No, I haven't, but I don't expect you to believe me."

"You are not giving away twelve and a half percent of my company!"

Viktor didn't know if Jeremy realized he'd just effectively taken the third prong of his threats off the table. No way was he going to allow Harry Grayson Sr. to own twenty-five percent of AIH.

Jeremy and Madison were too much alike.

Both would go to extreme measures for what was most important to them. The problem was that while Madison was very important to Jeremy, she did not believe it and Jeremy was willfully blind to what Madison needed from him.

Beyond that Archer International Holdings came first with Jeremy, and the people she cared about came first with Madison. Right now, those two priorities were in direct conflict.

Things were going to go completely pear-shaped if Viktor didn't take control.

"Sit down, Jeremy," Viktor instructed the older man in a tone that was respectful, but firm.

With a glare for his daughter, Jeremy returned to his seat.

"This meeting has derailed and I believe it is time to regroup."

Jeremy nodded.

Viktor stood and straightened his suit jacket before walking around the table and offering his hand to Madison. "Come with me."

"What are you doing, Viktor?" Jeremy asked, his expression considering.

The man knew that AIH sat near the top of Viktor's priority list, too. The company was the conduit for his own plans and no chance was he starting over because of the father-daughter issues of its owner.

"Madison and I have some things to discuss."

Steven frowned at him. "You are not the only candidate, you know. This contract was offered to four of us."

"I am the only one who matters."

An infinitesimal quirk of his boss's mouth said he knew that was true, but he said, "I believe that is up to Madison."

The lady in question made a sound of disparagement. "Right. If the decision is mine to make, I assume it's to be from the men you included in this meeting. One of whom was already engaged, another is old enough to be my father with a history of failed marriages and the other a complete stranger. And then there is Viktor."

"Maxwell Black is a man worth knowing."

While it might be true, Viktor didn't appreciate Jeremy pointing it out. Two half-Russian boys, raised to appreciate a culture not fully American, Maxwell and Viktor had grown up together, their families close, their goals similar.

Friends of a sort, but too alike for comfort, both men were determined to make their mark on the world, to be at the top of the food chain.

Because of the different paths they took to dominant positions in the business world, Viktor's and Maxwell's interests had not conflicted before today.

Thankfully, Madison didn't look impressed by her father's words.

She shifted so she could make eye contact with the CEO of BIT. "Mr. Black, do not be fooled by Jeremy's mistaken ignorance. Those articles are lies made up by a man I believed was my friend. Perry and I never had any sort of sexual relationship, much less a BDSM one."

The pain underlying her measured tones prompted Viktor to make some plans in regard Perry Timwater.

"I believe you." Maxwell's assurance proved he was every bit as intelligent as Viktor had always known him to be.

Madison relaxed infinitesimally. "Good."

"Regardless of the reason for our meeting, I would like to get to know you, Miss Archer." Maxwell, damn his hide, smiled charmingly at Madison. "You seem like an interesting person."

She inclined her head. "Thank you, but—"

"Don't dismiss the possibility of our compatibility out of hand," Maxwell interrupted her with another of his lady-killer smiles. "I bet I could teach you to like some of the things you've been accused of needing."

Madison's gasp said she was shocked by Maxwell's words.

Whether the words themselves or where he chose to speak them, Viktor didn't know and it didn't matter. *He* wasn't surprised. Maxwell played to his strengths and exploited the weakness of others.

Turning the lurid headlines into something forbidden but potentially exciting was a solid tactic for handling the current situation and the humiliation Madison had to be experiencing. Though she'd done nothing to let it show.

Unfortunately for Maxwell, Viktor wasn't going to let the ploy succeed.

Nothing was standing between Viktor and control of AIH. Not even Madison herself, but particularly not Maxwell Black.

Clearly upset with Maxwell's words, Jeremy made a sound of protest.

Before the older man could say anything Viktor was in front of Black, blocking his line of sight with Madison. "That is not something you are going to discuss here, or with Madison at all."

"You think not?" Black challenged back.

"I know not."

"I don't need your protection, Viktor," Madison said quietly from behind him.

He turned to face her, but didn't move so Black would have to stand and sidestep to see her. "Nevertheless, you have it."

She shook her head, whether in denial, or frustration, he didn't know.

"I'm nowhere near taking him up on his offer.

I'm pretty sure even the mildest form of that kind of relationship requires trust and I don't have any. Not for men, particularly men with the same priorities as Jeremy Archer. *Businessmen.*"

She made the word sound like a slur.

Viktor didn't believe her regardless. Madison trusted *him.* She always had; even if she no longer realized it.

And while Maxwell's words hadn't surprised him, Madison's willingness to meet them head-on did. But then maybe it shouldn't have. She'd already shown her willingness to stand against her father.

Maxwell got up, his pose too damned relaxed for Viktor's liking. Even less did he like the way the other man moved around him to face Madison. "I see."

"Good."

"Nothing in the contract states we must share a bedroom."

Madison's eyes flared with…was it interest?

Viktor cursed under his breath. "In order to receive the shares stipulated, Madison and her husband must provide an heir for Archer International Holdings."

Madison gasped, anger shimmering around her like electric currents.

Before she could say anything, Maxwell

shrugged. "There is always artificial insemination."

"While we live two entirely separate lives?" Madison asked in a tone Viktor recognized, but from the reaction of both Maxwell and her father, they did not.

Jeremy puffed up with renewed anger while the other Russian-American nodded with smug complacency. "Exactly."

"We would be married in name only?" she asked, the disgust levels rising enough that the others should have recognized them.

They didn't.

"No." Viktor was done with the verbal games.

Madison gave him a look like she was questioning his right to make the pronouncement.

"That sort of relationship would be too uncertain for the health of Archer International Holdings," Viktor pointed out.

Disappointment dulled the blue of Madison's azure gaze, but she masked the emotion almost immediately. Viktor cursed silently.

Her father, however, nodded vigorously. "Precisely."

"I think your daughter has already proven she is more than capable of her own decisions." Maxwell's admiration was annoyingly apparent.

"I won't sign the contract," Jeremy said in implacable tones.

The BIT CEO didn't look worried.

Madison's features had gone smooth with a lack of emotion once again as she stared at her father. "You believe I would agree to that kind of marriage?"

For once Jeremy seemed incapable of speech, perhaps realizing finally how little interest Madison would ever have in such a cold-blooded bargain.

"But then you believed the lies Perry spewed, didn't you?"

"I never said that." Jeremy's voice had an alien quality.

Realization of his colossal error in judgment in the handling of his daughter must be settling in, but being who he was, Viktor's boss wasn't going to back down, either.

Madison pulled her copy of the contract from the stack of papers in front of her and stood. "I assume you aren't going to do anything to mitigate Perry's lies."

"I have done it. Do you think this agreement is only about AIH? This is as important for you as it is the reputation of my company." Jeremy clearly believed what he said, but then Viktor had made sure his company's president saw things exactly that way. "Once you are married to a powerful man with an impeccable reputation, you can begin to live down your youthful excesses."

"My life has nothing to do with your company."

Viktor wasn't about to let the conversation degenerate further and there was only one direction it was headed if the two kept talking. Down.

"Conrad will put out a press release categorically denying all of Timwater's allegations," Viktor inserted before another word could be said.

The media fixer looked up from his tablet. "I will?"

Severely unimpressed with the man's lack of dedication to the protection of the company president's daughter, Viktor let Conrad see his displeasure. "You will do a hell of a lot more than that. If you'd been doing your job properly to begin with, this situation would not have happened."

"Protecting Miss Archer from her own excessive behaviors has never been in my job's purview," Conrad claimed in snide tones.

"Did you notice the loss of confidence in AIH articles in the online press this morning?" Viktor asked. "The first of which went live within thirty minutes of that tabloid hitting newsstands. Or did you think that was just a coincidence?"

The media fixer swallowed audibly and shook his head.

Jeremy didn't look too happy, either. He'd been too focused on using the current situation to bring his daughter into line, and had ignored the bigger picture. Something that was anathema to him.

"Your job is to protect the image of this company and anyone affiliated closely enough with it to impact our reputation in the financial community," Viktor reminded Conrad in a hard voice.

"Yes, sir."

"Maybe it's too much for you. Perhaps you'd prefer to move to a PR position working for a nursing home?" Viktor allowed the implication that was the only type of job Conrad would be able to get to hang in the air between them.

The usually unflappable media fixer paled, showing the man still had some of the intelligence he had originally been hired for. "I'm on it."

"You should have been on it at four-fifteen this morning after the scandal sheet went on sale."

Conrad didn't argue. He'd screwed up.

"I don't know what you spent this meeting doing on your tablet, but whatever it was, it wasn't as important as getting ahead of Madison's situation."

"I was writing the engagement announcement."

"I see. Not nursing homes then. Maybe you should be writing puff pieces for online dating sites," Viktor opined.

Nervous laughter filled the room and Jeremy made a sarcastic sound of approval, but it was Madison's genuine amusement that Viktor enjoyed the most.

"I'll need your signature on a civil suit against Perry Timwater," Conrad told Madison.

"No."

Viktor wasn't surprised by Madison's answer and forestalled any arguments from the media fixer or Jeremy. "The man was her friend. She's not going to sue him."

"Some friend." Conrad snorted.

The tiny wounded sound that Madison made infuriated Viktor. "We have other avenues of influence to bring to bear. I want a retraction from Perry in time for this evening's news. Play it off as a joke perpetrated by one friend on another."

Viktor turned to Madison. "For real damage control, you are going to have to do an in-person interview for one of the big celebrity news shows and meet with a journalist with a wider readership than the original article."

"Whatever I can do," she said with more conviction and none of the disagreement he expected.

Viktor's brow wrinkled in thought. Something about this scandal concerned Madison enough that she'd come to her father to ask for help.

While Jeremy might not see Madison showing up for this meeting as that, Viktor was certain of the truth.

Unlike her other escapades, Madison wanted this one cleaned up and her father's refusal to take it seriously had bothered her. A lot.

Viktor needed to figure out why it meant so much to her.

He put his hand out to her again. "Come with me, we'll talk your father's plan through and make some decisions from there."

She looked ready to argue.

He smiled at her. "Is that really too much to ask? I've got Conrad working on fixing this for you."

"Are you going to tell him to stop if I refuse?"

"No." Madison needed an act of good will.

It was important she realized that she could trust Viktor to watch out for her. He had to be the only candidate for her fiancé that she seriously considered.

Because her husband was going to take over AIH eventually and Viktor had every intention of that man being him.

Madison tucked her purse under her arm. "Okay."

"Just a minute," Jeremy said.

Viktor turned to face him. "I know what you want."

"But—"

"Have I ever neglected your interests in a negotiation?"

"No." Jeremy got that implacable look he was known for on his face. "Just remember that Madison's cooperation isn't the only thing on the line right now."

Viktor wasn't surprised by the threat, or even bothered by it.

He'd spent ten years working for this man and his ultimate goal was finally in reach. Viktor wasn't about to let it pass him by.

CHAPTER THREE

MADDIE FOLLOWED VIK into Le Mason, not at all surprised when the maître d' found them a table in a quiet corner in the perpetually busy restaurant, popular with tourists and locals alike.

"Did you eat breakfast?" he asked.

She shook her head, not even pretending to herself that shredding Romi's offering of chocolate pastries counted as actually ingesting calories.

He ordered the restaurant's specialty pancakes for her and coffee for himself.

"Did you bring me here to remind me of friendlier days?" she asked, sure she knew the answer.

"I brought you here because you used to crave their banana pancakes and I hoped to tempt you to eat." His six-foot-four-inch frame should have looked awkward in the medium-sized dining chair, but he didn't.

With his dark hair brushed back in a businessman's cut, his square jaw shaved smooth of dark stubble and a body most athletes would be jealous of covered in a tailored Italian suit, nothing about Viktor Beck could be described as awkward.

Doing her best to ignore his sheer masculine perfection, Maddie adjusted her napkin over her lap. "How did you know I hadn't already?"

"I guessed."

"I used to stop eating when I was stressed." She was surprised he remembered.

"Are you saying that's changed?"

"No." Too much was the same, but she wasn't about to tell him that.

She had to remember that Vik's interests here were aligned squarely with her father's. Not Maddie's. He'd made that clear six years ago and nothing had changed since.

Yes, Vik had gotten Conrad focused on curtailing the media frenzy around Perry's supposed breakup interview, but he'd done it for the sake of the company. Again...not Maddie.

Whatever his agenda now, it had the welfare of AIH as the end goal, she was sure of it. And if she got swept along with the tide, so be it.

"Give me the bullet points of the contract." She was morbidly curious about what her father had done to entice a man like Viktor Beck, or Maxwell Black for that matter, to marry her.

Vik's dark brows rose. "You trust me to tell you everything important?"

Answering honestly wouldn't just make a lie of her earlier words, but it would make her a fool. "I'll read it later to make sure."

"Your father accepts that you will not be his successor."

"What was his first clue?" She'd refused to get a degree in business and had fended off every request, demand and even plea for her to take a job at the company.

"Do you really need me to enumerate them for you?"

"No."

"Suffice it to say, Jeremy has finally accepted you are never going to be CEO of Archer International Holdings." Vik's deep tones were tinged with more satisfaction than disappointment at that pronouncement.

"It would certainly set a roadblock in your own career path if I were."

His espresso eyes flared with quickly suppressed surprise.

She smiled, pleased that he hadn't realized she knew. "You don't seriously think your desire for that office is a secret?"

"It's a family-owned company."

"That you plan to run one day and if Jeremy doesn't realize it, he's being willfully blind."

"That is one of his failings."

"You think?"

"He does not see you for who you are or what you need from him."

"You tried to tell him, once." The year before her clumsy attempt at seduction.

She'd thought Vik standing up for her meant he cared. But looking back, she had to conclude the friendship he'd offered her had been in pursuit of his own goals. Gaining Jeremy Archer's unmitigated trust.

She could have told Vik befriending her wouldn't do anything for him. Her father would have had to care about her for that to be the case. And he didn't.

The only thing that mattered to Jeremy Archer was the company. He'd married her mother to gain the necessary infusion of capital to make AIH a dominant player in the world market. His only interest in Maddie had been as a potential successor.

"He's given up on me personally because he realizes I'm never going to be his *business* heir." As much as it hurt, it also made sense of how unconcerned he'd seemed to be by "Perrygate."

"The only thing Jeremy has given up is his plan to try to lure you into the business."

Maddie shook her head, not buying it for a second. "You heard him. He had no intention of having Conrad help me until you stepped in."

"Your father can get tunnel vision."

"And all he could see was the endgame." He hadn't even noticed that her scandal had adversely impacted AIH's reputation.

"Yes."

Maddie waited for the waitress to place her pancakes on the table and walk away. "Which is?"

"You married to a man who can and will be groomed to take over as Jeremy's successor."

"If my father can't get what he wants out of me, he'll use me to get it, is that right?"

"That's a very simplified view and not entirely accurate."

She wasn't going to argue something she knew to be true, as did Vik, even if he was too loyal to admit it.

"Jeremy wants his successor to be family." Hence the marriage. "How old-fashioned."

"It ensures his grandchildren will inherit his legacy intact."

"And that's important."

"To him."

The smell of pancakes, fresh bananas and syrup had her mouth watering. "What about you?"

"You need to ask?"

"AIH is your life." As much as it had always been her father's.

"Say rather AIH is the vehicle for my own dreams."

"I didn't know men like you dreamed."

"Without visionaries at the helm, companies like AIH would atrophy and eventually die."

"So, you think my father is just a very dedicated dreamer." Sarcasm hanging thick from her words, she took a bite of her pancakes and hummed with pleasure.

Vik laughed. "That is one way to put it."

"And your personal dreams include being president of AIH one day."

"Yes."

His easy honesty surprised her and charmed her in a way. She'd always thought of men like him as having goals. Solid, steady, unemotional stepping stones that marked their success.

"Wow. I guess the heart of a Russian really does beat under that American-businessman veneer."

"My grandparents like to think so."

She offered him a bite of pancake with a slice of banana. "And your parents?"

Vik took the bite just like he used to and memories of a time when they'd been friends, and all *her* dreams had centered on this man, assailed Maddie.

"My mother has been out of the picture for all of my memory. My dad is like a computer virus. He keeps coming back."

She smiled. "I should say I'm sorry, but having a father who drives you nuts makes you more human."

Vik shrugged, but she couldn't help wondering if he'd told her about his dad on purpose. To build rapport. She thought Vik had outclassed her dad a long time ago in the manipulation department.

After all, Jeremy Archer still thought he ran AIH. However anyone with a brain—not blinkered by willful blindness—and access to the company would realize it was actually Vik's show and had been for a few years.

"Whose idea was it to offer Steven Whitley and Brian Jones up on the chopping block?"

"It's hardly a sacrifice to be offered this kind of opportunity." Vik drank his coffee, his expression sincere if she could believe it.

But then what was to say she couldn't?

"Marriage to the prodigal daughter for an eventual company presidency?" That might well be worth it to a man like Vik.

"You don't exactly fit the distinction of prodigal."

"Don't I?"

"You haven't blown through your inheritance. In fact, you are surprisingly fiscally responsible."

"Thank you, I think."

"You haven't abandoned your family to see the world."

"I moved out of the family home."

He winked at her. "But stayed in the city."

"What can I say? I love San Francisco."

"And your father."

"I'd rather not talk about that."

"Understood." He smiled and her nerve endings went *twang*. "Your media notoriety isn't even of the truly scandalous variety."

"Until Perrygate."

Vik waved his hand, dismissing the importance of Perry's lies. "That will be handled."

"Thank you for that." The thought of being forced to give up her volunteerism because of an unsavory reputation hurt deeply, compounding her pain at Perry's betrayal.

He knew how important working with the children was to her.

"But seriously?" she asked, refocusing. "Whitley and Jones?"

Vik shrugged, but his lips firmed in a telling line. "They're the most likely men within the company to do the job."

"Marrying me?"

"Becoming the next president."

"Besides you."

"Besides me," he agreed.

"You're the only *real* candidate."

"I would like to think so."

"And then there is Maxwell Black."

Vik's eyes narrowed, the brown depths darkening to almost black. "Your father is never going to approve the kind of marriage Black suggested."

"And if that is the only kind of marriage I'm willing to agree to?" she taunted.

"Jeremy will hire a surrogate and have his own child in hopes of succeeding with him where he failed with you."

Wholly unprepared for that answer, several seconds passed before Maddie felt like she could breathe again. "He's not a young man any longer."

"He is fifty-seven."

"He would not be so cruel." And she did not mean to her.

No child deserved to be born merely as a player on the chessboard. She should know.

She'd taken herself out of play, but she'd had the strength of the memory of her mother's love to bolster her own courage.

This child would only have Jeremy Archer.

Maddie shivered at the prospect. "I'm not having a child simply for him or her to be put in the same position."

"You want children." There was no doubt in Vik's voice.

"Someday."

"Whenever you have them, or whoever you have your children with, Jeremy will want the company to ultimately pass on to them."

"I know." Her father's role in her life and that of any children she might have was something she'd already spent several hours talking to her therapist, Dr. MacKenzie, about.

"That is not a bad thing."

She'd come to realize that. While Maddie's feelings about AIH were too antagonistic for her to ever want to be a part of it, as she'd always seen it as the entity that kept her father from her, it did not automatically follow that her children would feel the same way.

"You said something about me having a child being necessary for the man I marry to take over AIH."

"Upon the birth of our first child, my succession to the presidency will be announced. Your father will shift into a less active role as chairman of the board on his sixtieth birthday."

"And if I haven't had a child by then?"

"My becoming company president will not happen until we have had our first child."

"What if we can't have children?"

"We can."

"You sound very certain."

"I am."

She remembered the ultrasound her doctor had ordered as part of her last physical, at the company's request. She'd thought it was odd, but since her medical insurance was through AIH, Maddie hadn't demurred.

"Jeremy had them run fertility tests on me."

"Just preliminaries, but enough to know that aside from something well outside the norm, you should have no trouble conceiving."

"That's so intrusive!"

Vik didn't reply and, honestly, Maddie didn't know what she wanted him to say. She wasn't entirely sure the test had been all her dad's idea. If Vik had suggested them, she wasn't sure knowing would be of any benefit to her.

"What else?"

"The contract gives five percent of the company to me on our five-year anniversary. Another five percent on the birth of each child, not to exceed ten percent."

"How generous, he'll allow me to have two children." She'd always dreamed of having, or adopting, at least four and creating a home filled with love and joy.

"The contract does not limit the number of children you have, only the stock incentive to me for fathering them."

She ignored the way Vik continued to assume he was her only option. "What else?"

"On your father's death, if we have been married for ten years, or more, I will get another five percent of the company. The remaining fifty percent of the company will be placed in trust for our children with voting proxy passing only to our children actively involved in the executive level of running the company. I will hold all outstanding family-voting proxies."

"But the other children will receive the income from the shares."

"Yes."

"It sounds complicated." But then her father wasn't a simple man, not by any stretch.

Vik took a sip of his coffee. "Jeremy wants a legacy and you've made it clear you won't be part of it."

"So he wrote me out of the will."

"Only insofar as his ownership of Archer International Holdings is concerned."

"I see." Honestly, she didn't care.

The Madison Trust provided all the income she needed to live on. That income would decrease once half of her shares in the company transferred to Romi, but Maddie didn't mind.

The biggest expense she had was keeping up her appearance as Madison Archer, socialite. As far as she was concerned, that part of her life could go hang. If her father wanted her to keep up appearances, he could pay for the designer wardrobe and charity event tickets.

"Is there anything else pertinent to me in the contract?"

"Your father would like us to live in Parean Hall."

The Madison family mansion, named for the pristine white marble used for flooring in the oversized foyer and the risers on the grand staircase, had stood empty since the death of Maddie's grandfather from a massive coronary upon hearing of his daughter's accidental death nine years ago.

"I have plans for the house." It was part of the trust and would come to her when she turned twenty-five.

"What plans?"

"That is none of your business."

"Indulge me."

Maddie didn't answer, but concentrated on finishing her pancakes. Vik didn't press.

His patient silence finally convinced her to tell him.

She said, "I want to start a charter school, this one with boarders from the foster-care system."

"An orphanage."

"No, a school for gifted children in difficult family circumstances." A place the children could be safe and thrive.

Vik sipped at his coffee pensively for several moments.

"How will you fund it?"

"A large portion of my trust income will go to

it annually, but I also plan to raise funds amidst the heavy coffers of this city. I've learned a lot about fund-raising since my first volunteer assignment on the mayoral campaign when I was a teenager."

"Your father has no idea how full your life is."

"No, he doesn't." And Vik had barely an inkling as well.

She'd stopped telling him about her plans and activities when he'd rejected her so summarily six years ago.

Vik relaxed back in his chair. "The Madison family estate is a large house, even by the elite of San Francisco standards, but hardly the ideal location for a school. Either in building architecture or location."

"Oh, you don't think poor children should live among the wealthy?" she challenged.

He didn't appear offended at her accusation. "I think it will cost more than it's worth to get zoning approval."

"That section was zoned for the inclusion of a local school, but none was ever built."

"And you think that zoning will remain once your neighbors learn of your plans?" he asked in a tone that said he didn't.

"I don't intend to advertise them."

One corner of his lips tilted just the tiniest bit. "A fait accompli?"

"Yes."

"You have to apply for permits, hire staff…, it's not going to stay a secret long."

"And then the fight begins, you are saying?"

"Yes."

"But why should the residents care if there's a school in their neighborhood? The city planners clearly intended there to be one."

"And the fact there isn't should tell you something."

"But—"

"I can find you a better building."

She didn't want to sell her grandparents' home. Her memories there weren't the greatest. Her Grandfather Madison had often made Jeremy Archer look warm and cuddly by comparison, but Maddie's mother's stories of her own childhood had been filled with delight.

Maddie always wished she'd had a chance to know her grandmother, Grace Madison.

"I'll have to sell the mansion to finance another purchase." No matter how much she might not want to do it.

The school was too important to give up and Vik was right, as he so often was—the opposition to a boarding school in that neighborhood for the underprivileged was bound to be stiff.

Vik shook his head decisively. "I'll buy the other building."

"In exchange for what?"

"Consider it my wedding gift to you."

"Presumptuous."

"I'm the only man I will allow you to consider." Dark brown eyes fixed on her with unmistakable purpose.

She ignored the way his words sent shivers through her insides. "You're assuming I'll agree to marry."

"Your father doesn't realize it, but I know he didn't need anything beyond his first threat to convince you to fall in with his plans."

"You don't think so?"

"Are you in another relationship?" Vik asked, the words clipped, something like anger smoldering in the depth of his gaze.

"No." Maddie saw no reason to hedge.

"Dating anyone?" he pressed.

"No." She frowned. "Why are you asking about this now?"

"Because if you were in a relationship with someone who mattered to you, no pressure your father brought to bear would sway you into marrying someone else."

He was right, but it rankled. "You think you know me so well."

"I know that your dad means more to you than you want him to believe."

"It's not a matter of what I want." Her father

didn't think he mattered to Maddie because she wasn't all that important to *him*. Not in a personal way.

"Jeremy isn't going to back off on this."

"Why now?"

"You need to ask?"

"Yes." Her father had been too unconcerned about Perry's scandal for it to be what tipped him into must-get-my-wayward-daughter-married mode.

"Jeremy has been worried about what will happen when you come into your majority for the Madison Trust for a while."

"Now he knows."

"I don't believe he saw that one coming."

"No. It wouldn't have occurred to him that I would purposefully put Archer International Holdings at risk."

"No."

"But apparently the idea that I might marry someone who might do that had already occurred to Jeremy."

"Yes." Something about the quality of Vik's stillness said he might have had more to do with that than her own father's paranoia.

"So, he was already considering how to get me to marry the man of his choice?" Maddie surmised. "He's using Perrygate as a vehicle for his own agenda."

She wasn't surprised by her father's merce-
nary motives, but she didn't have to like them.

"You would have to ask him." Vik indicated
to the waitress to bring their bill. "I think the reality is more that he is afraid you'll end up with
Mr. Timwater. Your father will do anything to
prevent that."

"To protect the reputation and future of the
company." Considering Perry's poor luck with
his own business ventures, she could understand
her father not wanting him to get even shallow
hooks into any part of AIH.

"Sometimes, I think you are as willfully blind
as your father." Vik shook his head. "He wants
to stop you from marrying a man who would
go public with the kind of claims Perry made in
his interview."

"And Jeremy believes you're a huge improve-
ment."

"You don't?" Vik asked, his tone more than
a little sardonic.

She wasn't about to answer that. "Perry has
never been in the running."

"Several articles in the media over the past six
years would suggest otherwise."

"And the media *never* gets it wrong."

"You've never denied it, not publicly and not
to your father."

"That's where you are wrong." And she had

no satisfaction in that truth. "I told my father that Perry was just a friend, but he never believed me. He's always been more interested in his own interpretations and those of the media than anything I might have to say."

"I don't think that's true, but he is stubborn."

"So are you, in the way you defend him."

"Would you respect me if I had no loyalty for *my* friends?"

"Is my father your friend?"

"Yes." The single word wouldn't let her doubt his sincerity.

She used to think Vik was her friend, too.

Then things changed.

Now, she was facing the reality that it wasn't just that her father wanted her to marry Vik, but so did the man himself. Both had their reasons, but while different those reasons all centered around AIH, not Maddie.

She wasn't sure where, if anywhere at all, she came into the picture, other than as a minor piece on the chessboard. She certainly didn't feel like the queen.

CHAPTER FOUR

"I'LL BE BACK at three to take you to the lawyer's office," Vik informed Maddie as she unlocked her door and stepped inside.

"Are you sure that's not a conflict of interest?"

"Would you rather go alone?" he asked, a mocking twist on the masculine lips she'd spent far too much time studying as a teenager.

"No." Especially not after witnessing the media circus outside her building.

The paparazzi had always found her interesting, but it had never been like this.

And it was only getting worse as the morning wore on.

She'd managed to sneak out of the back entrance earlier, but the story and her location had spread in just that amount of time. There were almost as many media leeches haunting the other entrances to the building as in front now.

Even the parking garage hadn't been free of their presence.

She'd expected Vik to have his driver drop

her off, but she could only be grateful he had insisted on getting out of the car and escorting her all the way to her apartment door.

He'd kept his body positioned protectively between her and the reporters stalking her. Vik was also very good at remaining silent no matter what was thrown at them and Maddie found it easier not to react with him as a buffer.

"Security will have the parking garage cleared," Vik said after a short text conversation on the elevator.

"Thank you."

They stepped off the elevator into a thankfully empty hallway.

Vik looked both ways before leading her toward her door anyway. "You need a security detail."

She shrugged, not wanting to get in to this argument right now, and not at all sure she would win it.

"When was the last time you had this lock changed?" he asked as she opened the door.

She looked up at him, wishing it didn't feel like all the oxygen got sucked out of the air every time she did that. "Why would I have it changed?"

"At least tell me you had new locks installed when you moved in."

"Why would I?" she asked again. "I'm sure

the building management took care of it when the previous tenants moved out."

His expression said he didn't share her confidence. "You don't own the apartment?"

"No." She'd always planned to move into the mansion once she'd turned it into a school after she got control of her Madison Trust inheritance.

"Who has a key to this door, besides any previous tenant?" he asked with sarcastic emphasis on his last words.

Maddie leaned against the doorjamb when he showed no signs of following her inside. "Romi." She grimaced. "Perry, but he's not going to show his face."

Vik just shook his head before pulling his phone out and making a call. "Get the building access cards affiliated with Madison Archer's apartment deactivated and new cards issued for her, Ramona Grayson and myself."

He listened in silence for a moment. "Yes, have Ms. Grayson's delivered to her and the others to my office. I will pass Miss Archer's on when I see her later this afternoon. I want a security system installed, along with high-grade safety locks while we are gone."

The day before, Vik's high-handedness would have made Maddie livid. Today? It just felt like someone was watching out for her.

"You know, for a corporate shark, you're

pretty good at this white-knight stuff," she observed as he tucked his phone away.

"I make a good ally."

"But a terrifying enemy, I bet."

"You'll never have to find out."

"Even if I refuse my father's ultimatum?" She didn't bother to point out that if she did agree, she could still choose to marry a different man.

They both knew how unlikely that was.

Her youthful affections notwithstanding, she wasn't about to marry a stranger or a man who had multiple divorces under his belt.

Vik reached out and cupped her nape, stepping forward until mere centimeters separated their bodies, the heat from his surrounding her in a strangely protective cocoon. He didn't say anything, just caught her gaze, his dark eyes compelling her to some sort of belief.

Her breath escaped in a whoosh, unexpected and instant physical reaction crackling along her nerve endings while her heart started a *precipitando*. "Viktor?"

"You will never be my enemy, Madison."

"You're so confident I'll do what you want?"

"I'm confident *in* you, there's a difference."

There so was. He couldn't have said anything more guaranteed to get to her. People who believed *in* Maddie were a premium in her life. And less by one after this morning.

Dark espresso eyes continued to trap her even more effectively than his hand on her neck. "Trust me."

"Do I have a choice?" she asked with an attempt at sarcasm.

"No." His reply held no responding humor. Tilting his head, he stopped only when their lips almost touched. "You don't, and do you know why?"

"Tell me," she said in a voice that barely registered above a whisper.

"You already do." Then his mouth pressed against hers and the drumbeat in her chest went to the faster paced *stretto,* while electric pleasure sparked from his lips to hers.

A sensation she'd only known once before despite the fact she'd tried kissing other men. Six years ago when she'd thought the best way to celebrate becoming an adult would be to tell the man she'd been infatuated with for years that she loved him.

Even the memory of that old humiliation could not diminish the feelings of ecstasy washing over her from this elemental connection.

The kiss didn't last long, just a matter of seconds, but it could have been hours for the impact it had on her. When Vik pulled away and stepped back, Maddie had to stop herself from following him.

"Three o'clock. Turn your phone ringer off. I'll text."

She nodded, her mind blown by a simple kiss. Which did not bode well for her emotional equilibrium.

She fought acknowledging the possibility that tycoon Viktor Beck might well be more dangerous to the almost twenty-five-year-old Maddie as Archer business protégé Vik had been to her as a teenager.

"Go inside and lock the door, Madison."

She nodded again, but didn't move as she tried to reconcile the present with the past.

He shook his head, a curve flirting at the corner of the usually serious lines of his mouth. "You're going to be trouble."

"That's what my father says."

"I was thinking of a very different kind of trouble." Vik traced her bottom lip. "Believe me."

"Oh, really." Her lip tingling from his touch, warmth infused her that corresponded to the heat in his voice.

His smile became fully realized, and it was almost as good as the kiss.

She wasn't the one who was going to be *trouble*.

"Oh," she said again, this time without intending to, her body reacting to that warm expression in ways she just *didn't* with other men.

Vik waited in silence, no sense of impatience in evidence, but Maddie knew every minute he spent with her cost his tightly packed schedule.

She nodded to herself this time. "See you later."

Maddie stepped back into her apartment. Closing the door on him was a lot harder than it should have been.

She threw the dead bolt and a second later there was a double tap on the door. Vik's good-bye.

Using the pay-as-you-go cell phone she'd bought to provide Maddie Grace, volunteer, with a contact number, she called the school and let them know she wouldn't be in for at least a couple of days. She couldn't risk being caught in her Maddie Grace persona and having the best part of her life exposed to the media furor.

The next call she made was to Romi, who started cursing in French when Maddie told her friend that Jeremy Archer was using Perrygate to try to push Maddie into an *approved* marriage.

Maddie didn't tell Romi about the threat to her own father's company or Maddie's response to it. Romi would demand her friend not sign the papers.

"Are you going to do it? Are you going to marry the man you've been crushing on for the last ten years?"

"That was a schoolgirl crush. I'm twenty-four years old now."

"And still a virgin. Still avoiding relationships."

"I'm not exactly alone in that."

Romi's silence was as good as a verbal acknowledgment.

"Besides, I *could* marry one of the others."

"Right."

"Maxwell Black offered a marriage of convenience with children by artificial insemination." She couldn't help a small smile at the memory of her father's reaction to that offer.

She knew Romi would get a kick out of it as well.

"Max was part of your father's deal?" Romi demanded in a tone a couple of registers above her normal one.

All of Maddie's humor fled. "You know Maxwell."

Silence. "A little."

"More than a little if you call him *Max*."

"We went out a few times."

"You never told me."

"It's no big deal." But, threaded with vulnerability, Romi's tone said otherwise.

Maddie warned, "I think he found Perry's claims about our supposed sex life *intriguing*."

"I know."

"You what?" Maddie practically screeched,

her own problems forgotten for the moment. "How do you know that?"

"Do you really need me to spell it out for you?"

"You're still a virgin."

Romi had said so and the woman might be a hyperactive, borderline political anarchist and more than a little eclectic in her dress style, but she never lied.

"Technically, that is true."

"Technically?" Maddie drew the word out.

"Look, Maddie, I don't want to talk about it." Vulnerability now saturated Romi's voice, defenselessness that Maddie could not ignore.

"Okay, sweetie. But I'm here for you. You know that, right?"

"Always. SBC."

"SBC." Sisters by choice.

Maddie's mom had called them that the first time when she was explaining to the elementary school principal why the girls would do better with the same kindergarten teacher.

He'd refused to change their assignments and Helene Archer had called in the big guns.

It was the only time Maddie could remember her father stepping foot in her grade school. Mr. Grayson had come down, too, threatening to withdraw his company's support from the prestigious private school.

Romi and Maddie had never been assigned different classrooms again.

They had shared everything, including their grief at the loss of the only mother either girl had ever known when Helene Archer's speedboat had crashed into rocks invisible under the moonless sky.

Maddie hadn't gotten her propensity for risky behavior from nowhere.

She understood now that her mother's increasingly erratic behavior had been Helene's way of crying out for help. Help neither Maddie, nor her father, realized Helene needed.

It was a failure Maddie was still coming to terms with.

Vik's text came in at ten minutes to three.

He was on a conference call he could not reschedule, but two bodyguards would be at her door in a few minutes. They had AIH indigo-level security IDs and she was not to open the door unless she saw the familiar badges through her peephole.

Specially trained for protecting people rather than corporate property and secrets, the indigo team was her father's personal security detail. It used to be hers, too. Wanting to live as normal a life as possible, Maddie had refused to be assigned bodyguards when she moved out of the family mansion.

Her father had argued, but ultimately given in.

She didn't think Vik would be as easily swayed. If he thought Maddie needed a bodyguard for her security, she'd have one.

The same way the company's on-site security system had been upgraded because Vik deemed it necessary. Her father had been all for it, though.

Nothing was too good for Archer International Holdings.

The limo was waiting in front of the elevator bank in the parking garage. Thankfully, no enterprising reporter had managed to keep vigil. Which probably had less to do with the parking garage guards than the two additional indigo-badge bodyguards standing at attention on either side of the elevator doors.

One of them stepped forward to open the door to the limo and she stepped inside, only then realizing that Vik had taken the conference call on his mobile.

Every dark hair perfectly in place, his designer suit immaculate, he nodded at her while carrying on a conversation in Japanese.

His words did not falter, his Japanese smooth and unhesitating, and yet she felt the weight of his full regard. Like his attention was fully on her.

Like she mattered.

Succumbing to the desire to sit beside him, Maddie settled onto the smooth leather seat across from AIH's media fixer. Relieved that none of the bodyguards had instructions to join them in the back of the limo, she was still grateful the other occupant gave her an excuse to give in to the irresistible urge.

The need to be near Vik was verging on ungovernable, just like it had been six years ago.

Maddie wanted to chalk it up to the exceptional circumstances. She just wasn't sure she could.

Which was not enough of a caution to move to the other seat. There was simply no comparison between Vik and Conrad, who until that morning she had found slightly annoying but now considered flat-out obnoxious.

The PR guru took a break from typing madly on his tablet to silently acknowledge her. If his smile looked more like a grimace, she wasn't interested enough in interacting with him to call him on it.

Besides, Perry's fake exposé had triggered an ugly media frenzy beyond anything Maddie had ever experienced for her far more innocent escapades.

There was even speculation now that some of her riskier endeavors had been the result of orders from her *master*. That wasn't even the worst of it. Maddie did not know how a virgin could be labeled a sex addict with obvious intimacy issues, but she'd stopped reading her Google alerts after that headline.

The limo had exited the parking garage and pulled away from her building when Vik ended his phone call.

"Are you okay?" he asked Maddie.

Honesty would reveal a level of vulnerability she wasn't comfortable sharing with Vik, much less Conrad. She had no idea how her life had spun out of control so fast.

And Perrygate was only part of it. Her father's ultimatum and the realization their relationship would never be what she wanted had been followed too closely by the equally alarming, if for different reasons, acknowledgment that she was actually considering marrying her girlhood crush.

"I'm fine."

"Good," Conrad said, as if he'd asked the question. "Containing this media bloodbath is going to take serious effort and you need to be on your top game."

He didn't have to tell her. Maddie had spent the time since Vik had dropped her off earlier worrying about what would happen if she couldn't reclaim her reputation.

The all too real prospect of losing her dreams

of opening a small charter school tightened Maddie's throat, so she just nodded.

Once the media started looking more closely at Maddie's life, her alter ego was bound to come to light and the probability of losing her volunteer position was pretty much guaranteed.

While she enjoyed the anonymity of her Maddie Grace persona, she'd only taken rudimentary steps to keep her two lives separate. She wasn't James Bond, after all, just a socialite who craved time contributing as a *normal* person.

The only reason no one had cottoned on to Maddie Grace and Madison Archer being the same person before was that the news simply wasn't all that interesting. Or it hadn't been.

Her notoriety as Madcap Madison had been of the innocent variety, good for filler pieces in the social columns, but not salacious enough to really impact circulation numbers. Therefore *she* had not been interesting enough to be targeted by any serious digging.

She'd no doubt reporters were getting out their sharpest spades now. Perrygate was all that and a bag of chips for the gossipmongers.

The most painful part of Maddie's predicament was that it wasn't just her dreams on the line here; Romi was equally invested in the charter school.

Vik sent a text and then pocketed his phone.

"Our lack of an immediate response opened the door to other spurious claims from supposed former lovers."

Vik gave Conrad a look that left no doubt exactly who the VP of Operations for AIH blamed for that mistake.

Maddie felt no smugness at the media fixer being so obviously in the doghouse with Vik. Her life was too out of control to harbor even a hint of that, but she couldn't help the small thrill of pleasure at him taking her side.

From the moment he'd stepped in and ordered Conrad's cooperation that morning, Maddie had known she wasn't alone in facing the painful consequences of her onetime friend's betrayal.

Conrad tugged at the collar of his shirt. "We're working on retractions, but the best strategy for solidifying the prank angle is to give the media hounds another story."

"What do you mean? Like a two-headed baby from outer space, or something?" Maddie asked as her phone chimed to indicate a text from one of her select group.

Thinking it was Romi, she pulled out her phone and checked the message. It wasn't from her SBC; it was from Vik and said, You are not fine. We will talk. Later.

She texted back. If you say so.

Vik pulled his phone out and replied to her

text while speaking. "Or something. A glossy celebrity gossip magazine has already offered a two-page spread announcing our formal engagement in exchange for exclusive photos of a lavish, well-attended wedding reception."

"We're engaged now?" Had she missed something between the text convo and their in-person discussion?

Vik didn't answer, but waited in silence for her to come to her own conclusion.

"It's the best way to stop any more dirty snow falling in this avalanche," Conrad said unctuously.

"Dirty snow? Really?" she asked sarcastically.

"Do you have a better word for it?"

"Perrygate."

"Appropriate, but don't use it on your social networks," Conrad instructed her. "It implies a negative rift between you and Mr. Timwater. We're dismissing all this as a joke gone wrong."

"Then you can play it off as the bad joke that ruined a friendship. I won't play nice with Perry." She couldn't.

Conrad frowned thoughtfully. "It would be better for you to be seen as the forgiving friend. Waiting a few months to cut the man from your life will increase your popularity."

"I don't care."

"Timwater isn't coming within a hundred feet

of Madison, not even to apologize." Vik's voice brooked no argument.

And Conrad proved he was more intelligent than other evidence to the contrary because he didn't make one. "Fine. Fine." He started taking notes. "'The Prank That Ended a Friendship.' I can use that. We can spin the angle even. 'The Bad Joke That Almost Ended an Engagement.'"

Maddie looked at Vik. "Is he for real?"

Part of her knew this was the way things had to be, that Conrad was just doing his job, but having her life reduced to clichés and headlines was not fun.

"It's going to be okay, Madison." Vik pulled her cold hand into his own. "Trust me."

He had never hesitated to invade her personal space, or to touch her, though she'd never noticed him being so free with others. It was one of the reasons she'd convinced her eighteen-year-old self that Vik might return her feelings.

She'd realized later that the small touches were probably the result of the way his Russian grandparents had raised him. Maddie had figured she hadn't seen him behave that way with others because he had so few personal relationships.

None but his grandparents and her father that she'd ever actually come into contact with.

That was one thing she and Vik had in common.

A very small inner circle.

She didn't comment on this now, just gave thanks for the fact he was willing to offer her the kind of comfort she needed and had never been able to ask for.

Vik squeezed her fingers. "Conrad is one of the best in the business. Before this morning I would have said *the* best."

Conrad flinched, proving he'd been listening even as he typed.

"And our engagement is the only way to restore my reputation?" she asked almost rhetorically.

She didn't see another way out, either.

Her father had more leverage for his plan than he could possibly comprehend. The realization of Maddie and Romi's dreams relied on a reputation Maddie could not afford to lose.

Vik frowned. "I'm sorry, Madison, but nothing is going to make the story go away completely."

"Why not?" Media fixers worked miracles.

Isn't that what everyone said? If they couldn't fix this, her and Romi's dreams were going to crash and burn. There was no way Maddie was going to let that happen.

Conrad looked up from his tablet. "Some people will always believe that where there is or was smoke, there had to be some ember of fire."

"But there isn't one."

The twist of Conrad's lips said he was probably one of *those* people.

Vik's hand moved to Maddie's thigh, bringing her attention careening back to him and him alone. "I believe you."

"No matter what the press has claimed, I've never even had a serious boyfriend," she admitted painfully.

Something flared in Vik's eyes, but he just nodded. "You've been too busy getting into trouble."

"Not *this* kind of trouble."

"I know."

"And not even my usual in the last six months."

Conrad's head snapped up. "Is that true?"

"I haven't done anything zany or even remotely newsworthy since I broke my pelvis in that botched skydiving landing."

Conrad narrowed his gaze. "What about parties? Random hookups?"

"Did you not hear her, Conrad?" Vik asked, dropping the temperature in the limo with the ice in his tone. "Madison does not do random hookups."

"She said she hasn't had a serious relationship, that the men claiming to have engaged in BDSM encounters are lying. Miss Archer never claimed to be celibate." Okay, so Conrad *had* been listening.

Vik didn't thaw even a little. "You can take *no random hookups* as a given."

"Can I?" Conrad asked Maddie, surprising her with his tenacity.

"Yes," she replied firmly. "I haven't been out in the evening except to attend charity events since my accident."

"With Perry as your escort?" Conrad asked, sounding unhappy by the possibility.

Which she could understand, in light of recent events. She wouldn't call the emotion she was feeling right now unfettered joy, either.

"A couple of times."

Vik's jaw hardened.

"Most events, Romi and I go together. Perry isn't all that interested in helping others." Maddie felt disloyal admitting that truth, but Romi had always said it.

Perry had never been as interested in the causes Maddie supported as the A-listers and potential business contacts he could meet at certain events.

"You've been at most of them, yourself," she offered to Vik.

He frequently represented AIH at that sort of thing, being an expert at making connections Perry only aspired to. Maddie knew that Vik also supported the causes in very tangible ways, both on behalf of the corporation and personally.

The gorgeous, corporate white knight nodded.

"That could work in our favor, unless you were photographed with your date for the evening," Conrad mused. "Even then, we could make it work."

"Vik hasn't had a date with him at one of these events in over a year." Knowledge that revealed how much attention Maddie paid to Vik.

A fact she'd done her best to hide even from herself, darn it.

His raised brow and knowing look said he realized that, too.

"That's good. We can back-engineer a budding relationship you've taken pains to keep out of the media spotlight." Conrad took more notes on his tablet. "This works."

Maddie turned toward Vik. "We're really getting married?"

"You tell me."

"Only it doesn't seem possible." Everything since her nearly spilled cup of coffee that morning felt like a dream, at times odd, unpleasant and bordering unbelievable.

"Believe it," Vik said, unconsciously answering her silent thoughts.

She narrowed her eyes, trying to read him. "How can you take this so calmly?"

"What am I supposed to be upset about?"

"Yesterday you were a free agent. Today you are engaged." Didn't that bother him, even a little?

Or was it something Vik had planned all along? Somehow, she couldn't quite dismiss that possibility.

"We are not engaged yet."

Something went tight in her chest. "But—"

"We will finish this discussion after you meet with the lawyer."

What did that mean? Did he think they were engaged, or not? *Were* they engaged? Had she said *yes?* She was pretty sure she hadn't. And she might know her choices were very limited, but did Vik? Really?

He returned his attention to his phone and sent a text.

This time she had no doubts it was to her.

Sure enough a few seconds later, her phone chimed. Trust me.

Trust him. Right. He thought it was that easy? "You aren't going to try to talk me out of signing the paperwork?"

"I told Jeremy threatening Romi could boomerang on him."

"He didn't believe you."

"He has a hard time backing off once he's set a thing in motion."

"Are you saying he's already started the wheels

of destruction for Mr. Grayson's company? They used to be good friends."

Vik shrugged noncommittally. "He's done the research on how to make it happen."

"And he didn't want to waste his efforts?" Her dad could be so cold, but then that wasn't breaking news.

"You and I have agreed Jeremy could have no idea how spectacularly it would come back to bite him on the ass."

"But you aren't trying to change my mind."

Conrad stopped typing and listened as if he, too, was curious about what was motivating Vik's behavior.

Vik ignored the other man, his focus entirely on Maddie. "Those shares ultimately belong to you."

"My father doesn't see it that way."

"It never occurred to Jeremy that any child of his would consider AIH as a means to an end rather than the end itself."

What did he know? Did Vik realize she had always intended to use her income from the shares to run the school?

It wouldn't be a long stretch from what she'd told him that morning.

What he couldn't know was that Romi would do the same. She wanted the school as much as Maddie.

Vik's dream was something quite different, but obviously just as important to him. "You want the company."

"Like your father, I want to leave a legacy for my children." Some might think the lack of emotion in Vik's deep tones belied his words.

Maddie knew better.

His dark brown eyes burned with certainty. "Archer International Holdings will be that legacy."

"But we're not engaged." She couldn't help the small bit of sarcasm.

Maddie was unsurprised by Vik's lack of response.

CHAPTER FIVE

MADDIE'S TIME IN the lawyer's office went quickly, though the elderly man did ask if she was sure she knew what she was doing.

Maddie had no doubts.

Vik stood when she came back into the anteroom, no sign he was in any way upset about what she'd been doing. "All finished?"

"Yes."

"Do you have any plans for the rest of today?"

"No."

Vik put his hand on the small of her back and walked with her out of the law office. "Good."

"Why?"

"We have a photo shoot with the magazine photographer this evening. He'll join us for dinner at your father's mansion. My grandparents will be there."

"Playing happy families? Is that really necessary?"

"Yes."

When they reached the parking garage, he led

her to his car, the limo and SUV full of bodyguards nowhere in evidence.

"Conrad is in the limo with a redheaded decoy." Vik opened the passenger door of the black amethyst Jaguar XJL for Maddie.

She settled into the luxury car. "Better her than me. I would have made a lousy celebrity."

"You think?" he asked. "Your father thinks you've been doing your best to become the next reality TV star."

"Just Madcap Madison, version two-point-oh."

Vik's expression went from smile to grimace, reflecting Maddie's own conflicting feelings about her mom's escapades in the light of adulthood. "In many ways Helene Madison Archer was an amazing woman and she raised a strong and impressive daughter, but the way she chose to cope with the things she didn't like in her life wasn't healthy. You must see that."

"I do." It had taken some time, but Maddie had come to that conclusion a while ago. The *Madcap* was something Maddie was doing her best to drop from her name. "Believe it, or not, I've always been very careful what part of my life I allow the media into."

"Perry isn't so choosy."

Vik was in the driver's seat, their identity obscured behind the Jaguar's tinted windows, when she replied. "Perry is an idiot who relied on our friendship to protect him from the consequences of his lies."

"It is."

"You think so?" She indulged in an old favorite secret pastime as he drove out of the financial district and through Chinatown toward Van Ness.

Watching Viktor Beck.

Memories of their recent kiss played over in her mind, a mental movie she could not seem to turn off and that caused a visceral reaction in her body. A reaction she wasn't sure if she should try to suppress, or not.

If they were getting married, reacting to his kiss was a good thing, right?

Thankfully, she didn't have to answer the disturbing question of whether she would marry him for the sake of her dreams if she *wasn't* attracted to him. How much of her father's ruthlessness colored Maddie's spirit?

She was sure Jeremy Archer would say the papers she'd just signed answered that question, but that wasn't how she saw it.

Vik shifted down, his car purring as it climbed the hills of San Francisco's streets. "You refuse to sue Perry despite his defamation of your character."

"Our friendship is over." Ultimately that would cost Perry more than any settlement she might get in court.

"Is it?"

"Yes."

"You sound very certain." Vik didn't.

"I am."

Vik turned onto Highway 101. "Good."

"And even if for no other reason than that he'll never get another loan from me, that's a serious consequence for Perry." One she really didn't think the other man had foreseen. He would have counted on her loyalty, but had made the egregious error of not giving her any. "He'll also never again be able to use being my escort as a way into events his own connections won't provide entrée."

"It sounds like it was a pretty one-sided friendship."

"That's what Romi always said, but it wasn't true."

"Yes?" Vik sounded genuinely curious, if doubtful.

"Letting people in isn't easy for me."

The business tycoon who had spurred more fantasies than any teenage heartthrob in her adolescent breast made a disbelieving sound. "You have a huge social network."

"And a total of two people I called friends, now only one."

"I think two still." Vik flicked her a glance with meaning. "Just not the same two."

Unexpected and not wholly welcome warmth

unfurled inside Maddie at the claim. Nevertheless, she admitted, "I'm glad to hear that."

She just hoped it was true. Chances were good. Viktor Beck might be a bastard in the business world, but he was no liar.

"He made me laugh," she admitted, falling back on old habits of sharing her uncensored thoughts with Vik.

"You have an infectious laugh," Vik offered. "I missed it."

It was weird to think of Vik missing anything about her. "You decided our friendship was over."

"Not over, just truncated."

"If you say so." But six years on, she could maybe share his point of view.

"I thought it for the best."

It was entirely possible it had been, no matter how much his rejection and subsequent pulling away had hurt. She hadn't thought so at the time, the combined loss of her mom, then her grandfather, what little attention she'd had from her father and then Vik's friendship had left Maddie with real intimacy issues. But if she and Vik had maintained their close friendship, she never would have gotten over him.

Nor would she have made her own way in life, building dreams completely independent of AIH.

"Looking back on it, it's kind of surprising I

let Perry get so close." But then she'd needed a replacement for Vik at least.

"You loaned him money."

Which had taken their friendship into a different realm, she now realized—a realm where Perry saw Maddie as a resource rather than a friend. "In the interest of accuracy, we'll have to call them gifts, not loans."

"And that makes it better?"

She shrugged, though Vik's attention was on the road as they joined the heavy traffic over the Golden Gate Bridge. "Perry's business ventures never seemed to work out."

"Selling this story to the tabloids is pretty stupid as a long-term plan if you were already bank-rolling him."

"I wasn't. I turned him down the last time he asked for money." It had been a hard decision, but she'd had her own dreams to bankroll. "I'd come to the conclusion there were better places I could sink my money than down the rabbit hole of another one of Perry's unlikely business ventures."

"So, he betrayed you."

"Yes." She sighed sadly. "I had no idea my friendship was only worth a few dollars."

"Fifty thousand."

"That's how much he got paid?" She wasn't surprised Vik knew.

The man made it a habit to know everything of even peripheral importance to him. Maddie figured it would be a matter of days, if not hours, before he learned of her anonymous volunteering and even her therapist.

Uncertainty about his reaction to her secrets was the only thing stopping her from telling him herself.

"For the initial tabloid article. He planned to leverage the scandal into more paid interviews and even a book deal." Vik's voice was laced with disgust.

"That's ridiculous. I'm not exactly a celebrity." She hated this.

"No, but you are the Madcap Heiress."

"Madcap Madison. It's what they called my mother." She could still remember the first time one of the tabloids had used the moniker for Maddie.

It had made Maddie feel like maybe Helene was still with her in some small way. Only later had her own maturity and help from her therapist helped Maddie to see how distorted that thinking was.

"You share her penchant for making it into the press," Vik agreed. "Perry's book wouldn't have made him a million dollars, but someone would have paid him a hefty advance for it."

"That's just stupid."

"That's our reality-television, celebrity-drama-obsessed society." Vik shifted into the higher gear as they finally made it over the bridge.

San Francisco's gridlock could get really ugly, though it was better than the freeways that became parking lots during high commute times in and around L.A.

"I suppose. You talk about the book deal like it's in the past."

"It is." Definite satisfaction colored Vik's two-word answer.

She shouldn't be surprised Vik had worked so quickly, but she couldn't deny being impressed and only a little apprehensive. "What were Perry's terms?"

"Timwater didn't set the terms, trust me."

She had no trouble believing that, not when Vik was involved. Perry had no hope with the power of AIH brought to bear against him at the instructions of its VP. "What did Conrad get him to agree to?"

"Do you think, after his screwup this morning, I would trust this negotiation with Conrad?"

"*You* met with Perry? Wasn't that overkill?" Putting Vik and Perry in the same room was like pitting an alley cat against the heavyweight champ.

The cat might be wily and street smart, but he was still going to get pulverized.

And she wasn't entirely convinced of Perry's street smarts.

"From now on, anything to do with you goes through me personally." Vik exited the freeway, downshifting the powerful Jaguar.

"That's not how my father operates."

They were headed toward the Marin Headlands. Maddie recognized the route, though she hadn't been there since her school days, on the obligatory field trip to the Golden Gate Bridge and to view the city vista.

"I am not your father."

"But you're a lot alike."

"In how we do business? Yes. But you share more personality traits with your father than I do."

"You're kidding."

"No."

"I know we're both stubborn, but…"

"It does not stop there, believe me."

"So you say." She was *nothing* like her father.

"I do."

Typical. Vik felt no need to explain himself, or convince her, which only made her want to hear his justifications all the more. She wasn't going to ask, though.

Not right now.

Right now, she was far more interested in what they were doing in the parking area near Battery

Spencer. "Is the magazine photographer here to get some color shots, or something?"

"No."

Vik pulled neatly into a parking spot and turned off the car, but made no move to get out.

He unbuckled his seat belt and turned to face her. "It is a good thing the friendship is over from your side. Timwater signed a nondisclosure agreement that covers every aspect of his association with you. The penalties for breaking it are severe."

"But he's going to talk about our friendship." It had spanned the same six years as the dearth of Vik in her life.

"No, he is not."

She had no desire to see the man again, but she wasn't sure how she felt about their friendship disappearing as if it had never been, either. "It isn't going to help with what he's already done."

Vik's eyes bored into hers. "He's signed a retraction, admitting everything he told the tabloid was a lie."

"Won't that leave him open to a lawsuit from them?" And why was she worried about someone who had so very blatantly not been worried about her?

"They don't get a copy of the confession… unless he screws up again." The threat in Vik's words would have been spelled out to her ex-friend in no uncertain terms.

"And that will protect him?"

"Do you care?"

"I probably shouldn't."

"You would not be you if you didn't," Vik said with something like indulgence and no evidence of judgment.

"I'm not a pushover."

"No one witnessing you facing your father down in the conference room this morning would ever question that."

"Okay."

Vik smiled. "You are a strong woman whose strength is tempered by compassion. My grand-mother Ana is such a woman."

"And you love her."

"Yes."

Did that mean he might love Maddie one day? She did her best to quash that line of fantasy thought. Like she'd told her father earlier, Maddie wasn't the fairy-tale believer her mom had been. She had no expectations of marrying for undying love and irresistible passion.

So, she couldn't understand where the tiny ember of hope burning deep in her heart despite Maddie's strictest self-talk came from.

Unaware of the war going on inside of Maddie from that simple admission, Vik added, "Tim-water will make a public apology for his prank after our engagement is announced."

Even though they *weren't* engaged, according to Vik.

It suddenly occurred to her that they hadn't come to the overlook for privacy to discuss Perry.

Even so, she needed to know one thing. "How much?"

"Did we pay him?"

"Yes."

"The way his apology will play, he'll get to keep his fifty thousand from the tabloid." Vik didn't sound particularly happy about that fact.

"And?"

"The only thing I gave Timwater was my word not to destroy his name in the business world. The nondisclosure agreement guarantees we will not sue him in civil court, either—so long as he keeps his side of it."

"He never would have believed I would do that."

"I would. Regardless of if it was on behalf of the company rather than you, Timwater would be just as screwed."

"You're ruthless."

"It's not just an Archer family trait. We do what we need to get what is important to us."

"Like marrying the owner's daughter to take control of a Fortune 500 company."

"Yes."

"Thank you."

"For?"

"Not trying to pretend this is something else." No matter what her heart wanted.

"What exactly do you think this is?"

"Necessary."

He nodded. "Yes, but it will be a marriage in every sense of the word. You do realize that?"

"You mean…"

"Sex. We will not be living celibate lives."

"No affairs?" Not that she would be willing to take this step if she thought he was a womanizer, if she herself had plans to look outside the marriage for that kind of companionship.

"No affairs," he repeated, making no attempt to suppress how disgusting he considered the idea.

Vik wasn't that guy.

He *was* the grandson of a very traditional Russian man. Vik would never do anything that would disappoint the old man. He thought his father had done enough of that.

He'd shared that, and a lot more she hadn't expected him to, when they were friends during her teen years. He'd never been like a brother, but he had been one of the few people she'd believed she could rely on back then.

Could she rely on him now?

"Be very sure you understand what I am saying here, Madison." Vik reached across the console and cupped her nape in a move that was becoming familiar. "I am not Maxwell Black. My children will not be conceived in a test tube."

"Of course not." Whatever their feelings for each other, this situation was very personal for him.

He nodded like that had settled everything still left unsaid between them. She wasn't so sure she agreed, but she didn't hesitate to get out of the car with him.

They took the path to the overlook, Maddie grateful she'd worn the sensible pumps and that the ground was dry. Neither of them spoke while they walked, but he kept his hand on the small of her back, moving it to her elbow in the uneven patches of terrain.

When they stopped, they were at one of the favorite overlooks that gave a view of both the famous bridge and the San Francisco skyline. A few tourists dotted the area, but none near enough to hear any discussion she and Vik might have.

Vik maneuvered them so he stood only a few inches from her, his body acting as a barrier against the incessant winds off the harbor. The close and clearly protective positioning felt significant.

"My grandfather gave my grandmother her first view of San Francisco in this very spot," Vik said after a moment of silent contemplation of the vista before them. "He promised her a future with food to put on the table for their family. A future without oppression for their Orthodox beliefs."

"He kept his promise."

"Yes." Vik went silent for several seconds of contemplation. "Grandfather brought my dad up here as a child. Misha told Frank he could be anything he wanted to, a true American with no accent, his name just like all the other boys'."

"Your grandfather gave your father the freedom to be anything he wanted to."

"Even a failure."

She couldn't argue that assessment, not when she knew Frank Beck had spent his adulthood running from responsibility. Unless something had changed in the last six years, Frank only contacted Vik when he wanted something. Usually money.

Placing her hand on his forearm, Maddie said, "He didn't fail when he fathered you."

"Misha and Ana raised me to be who I am."

"An undisputable success."

Vik turned to face her. "You believe that?"

"I do."

"That is good."

She smiled, not sure why she felt the need to reassure Viktor Beck, but determined to do it anyway.

"*Deda* brought me up here, too, when I was boy. Frank could not be bothered, but I made promises to myself, commitments to the children I would one day father. Promises *I* will keep."

"I have no doubt."

Vik's gaze warmed, his expression filled with unmistakable determination. "My grandparents were not in love when they married, but theirs is one of the strongest marriages I have ever witnessed."

"They are devoted to each other."

"And to their family, even my dad."

"I believe it."

Vik nodded, his dark eyes reflecting approval of her words. "That kind of dedication runs in my veins right along with the ruthlessness."

"I know."

Vik laid his big hands on her shoulders, creating a private world of two for them. "I believe our children will share those traits."

"No doubt." There was nothing she could do about how breathless her voice had become.

He was touching her, and even through the fabric of her Valentino suit jacket and the shell she wore under it, she felt the connection intimately.

"Considering it will come from both their mother and their father, our children have little hope otherwise."

"I'm not ruthless," she said, shocked by the accusation.

"The paperwork you signed today would say otherwise."

"You know that isn't the way I usually do things." It just had been...necessary.

"Ruthlessness does not have to be the dominant trait in your nature for you to have it."

"And it doesn't bother you?"

"That you'll fight for those who deserve your loyalty, even those who do not? No."

"You expect to deserve my loyalty."

"Yes."

"And will I get yours?"

His expression said her question surprised him. "Do you doubt it?"

"Six years ago..."

"You kissed me and I pushed you away."

"That's a simplified way of looking at it and not entirely accurate."

"No?"

"No. I told you I loved you. You told me I was too young and you didn't just push me away, you pushed me out of your life completely. Our friendship ended with one kiss."

"It was necessary."

"We could have stayed friends."

"No."

"Why not?"

"You were an eighteen-year-old, barely a woman."

"But I was a woman."

"I know." There was a message in his voice she couldn't decipher.

"You were also the daughter of a man I admired and who trusted me with you."

"Not to mention he was your boss," she reminded him a little snidely.

"Yes, my boss. The president and owner of a company I intended to run one day."

"A relationship with me would hardly have gotten in the way of *that* goal."

"It would have. Six years ago."

"But not now." No, *now* it was the opposite.

Marriage to her would give Vik exactly what he wanted.

"No, not now."

"I loved you." She wouldn't call it a crush; it hadn't been by then. She'd gotten over it, but at one time she *had* loved him. "Your rejection hurt me."

"I am sorry."

But he wouldn't change his past actions, even if he could. She knew him.

"Look on the bright side," he said almost teasingly.

She didn't remember anything bright about that time. "What?"

He smiled like a shark. "It should be easy for you to learn to love me again."

"Emotion doesn't work like that." And she was pretty sure falling in love with this man, even if she married him, wouldn't be the smartest thing she could ever do.

"Doesn't it?" He pulled something out of the inside pocket of his coat. A small lacquer box that fit in his palm. "My grandmother brought this *Palekh* over from Russia when she and my grandfather defected during the Cold War."

"It's beautiful."

"It is a reminder."

"Of what?"

"The beauty they left behind and the life they hoped to build. *Deda* always said *Babulya* was his frog princess."

The top of the box was decorated with an image from the Russian fairy tale where Prince Ivan ended up married to an industrious and lovely princess who had once been a frog. The magical princess outdid her aristocratic counterparts set to marry Ivan's brothers in every way.

Maddie thought maybe she understood why Vik's grandmother Ana had told Maddie the story of the frog princess the first time they'd met.

"Does this make you my frog prince?" she asked tongue in cheek.

Vik traced the rich image painted in egg tempera on black. "Perhaps it does."

"You know I don't believe in fairy tales."

"Maybe you should."

Now, *that* was definitely *not* something her father ever would have said to her.

"Your grandfather's promises seem to fly in the face of Russian pessimism." But then Misha Beck had never struck her as a pessimist.

The man who had changed his last name to reflect his new country and life had a decidedly forward-thinking attitude.

Maddie had only met Vik's grandparents a few times, but she liked them.

A lot.

Despite the fact Misha and Ana had raised their grandson, Maddie had always considered them the epitome of a *normal* family. The kind of family she'd always wanted.

The kind she wasn't sure Vik was offering with whatever was in that small lacquer box.

"*Deda* never believed the old adage that to speak of success cursed it." Though his shoulders didn't move, there was a shrug in Vik's voice.

"His life and yours prove his skepticism."

"That is one way to look at it."

"The other?"

"*Deda* gave up being a Russian and embraced the way of his new homeland."

"The American ideology does tend toward the positive."

"Remember that."

"You think I have to be a dreamer because of where I was born and raised?" she demanded.

"No. You have your dreams. I have mine. It is not about where you were born, but who you were born to be. I want you to believe in both of our dreams."

"And that takes some of the idealism this country is known for."

"Yes."

He wanted her to believe in his dreams.

It might be love between them, but this was more than a business proposal—no matter what had prompted it.

CHAPTER SIX

"AND THIS?" SHE pointed to the *Palekh* that had to be at least fifty years old. "Is it a reminder for *me* now?"

No matter how unmoved she tried to appear about that possibility, it touched her deeply.

"Yes."

Her breath hitched. "Of the successful legacy you promised your unborn children?"

"Among other things."

"That kind of success is more important to you than it is to me." Maddie wanted promises of other things.

She wasn't naive. She wasn't looking for undying love, despite the odd feelings deep in her heart she was doing her best not to acknowledge. Even Helene Archer had been too pragmatic to promise her princess a knight in shining armor that would *love* Maddie. But there was more to life than building a company that dominated the world market.

"You think so?" he asked, sounding amused.

Though she didn't understand why. Maddie could only nod.

"It will take the *significant* results of that type of success to make your school a reality."

She couldn't deny it.

"You think money means little to you, but then you have never lived in fear of want." If he had sounded even a little condescending, she would have been angry.

He didn't.

"And you have?" she asked, wondering if there was something about his past she didn't know.

"Not like my grandparents, but let's just say the year between my mother's death and *Deda* deciding I would come to live with him and *Babulya* was not one I would ever allow my own child to endure."

"I'm sorry."

"Frank's inability to make anyone's needs as important as his own, including the basic need to eat of his six-year-old son, taught me as much about who I did not wish to be as *Deda* taught me about the man I would become."

"Your grandfather is a good man."

"He and *Babulya* raised me with an appreciation for the difference between working to provide and working an angle."

"Like your dad."

Vik grimaced. "Frank is very good at angles."

"You want your life to matter."

"It already does."

She couldn't argue that. Didn't want to. "I want my life to matter, too—we just have a different way of going about it."

"Yes, we do." He didn't sound bothered by that fact.

Why was she?

She wanted to tell him about Maddie Grace, but wasn't sure how she would handle it if Vik had the same attitude about her efforts as Jeremy had had.

"I have already promised to help you see your dream of a charter school realized," Vik pointed out.

Yes, he had, which put Vik miles ahead of her father in that regard already. Maybe their differences would make both of their lives better, rather than tearing them apart.

"What kind of promises are you making with that box, Vik?" she asked, almost ready to believe in the possibility of the complete family she'd never had.

His handsome lips tilted a little at the nickname she hadn't uttered in six years, keeping it strictly private to her thoughts. Something she had not been able to let go of, but would not share with others, either.

"If you accept my proposal, I promise fidelity."

She nodded.

"I will expect the same," he said, as if there was any chance she didn't already realize it.

Interesting that he'd led with that one, though. Was that because he thought she needed it after Perry's betrayal, or was it more personal for Vik?

Either way, she said, "That's a given."

"I am glad to hear that."

When he said nothing else, but looked down at her with an expression that seemed to see into her soul, Maddie prompted, "And?"

"I promise to continue to grow AIH, leaving our children a legacy worthy of both my family and yours."

It was a promise meant more for and to himself and their future children, but she didn't dismiss it is as unimportant. Not after he pointed out her own dreams required money just like his did, if not on the same scale. "All of our children?"

"Yes." His brow furrowed. "Why would I distinguish?"

He could be one of those men who considered their eldest their only important child, or only their sons. But she knew he wasn't.

Her concerns were a lot more unpredictable.

"I am willing to have two children with you, but I want more and they will be adopted." This wasn't a deal breaker for her.

Not if she could have her school, but it was

something she desperately wanted to do. Be open to the possibility of bringing children into her life that they could offer a family, not just support, encouragement and help.

Vik's brows drew together in thought, not a frown. "You want to adopt?"

"Yes."

"Babies or children?" he asked.

"Does it matter?"

"No."

Happy with that answer and the speed of it, she offered, "Most likely children."

"All right."

"That's it? You agree?" Shock coursed through her.

"I assume we will make any decisions in regard to bringing more children into our lives—both those born to us and adopted by us—together."

"Of course, but you're open to it?"

"Nothing would delight Misha and Ana more than a house full of grandchildren to spoil."

"There are a lot of bedrooms in Parean Hall." Which was her acquiescence to living there as a married couple.

His satisfied smile said he recognized that as well. "I do not anticipate filling them all with children, but have no objections to our family inhabiting half of them."

It was a ten-bedroom mansion.

Could it really be this easy? "You'll put that in the prenup?"

"If you insist, but I assure you it is not necessary." He placed the antique Russian keepsake against her palm. "Any promises I make you here will not be broken."

"So long as it is within your power."

"Yes." His tone and expression implied Viktor Beck considered very little outside his power and influence.

"And you will be a father to our children, not just the man with that title." He wasn't the only one with memories of neglect after the death of a mother.

Hers might not have been to her physical needs, but Jeremy Archer had let Maddie starve emotionally.

"I cannot promise to make every Little League game or sit-in your daughters organize, but I will make our children a priority."

"*My* daughters?"

"Mine will be too busy trying to take over the corporate world for social activism."

Tickled, she laughed like she hadn't with him in too long, but grew serious again quickly enough. "I won't have my child forced into dedicating his or her life to AIH. That has to be a personal decision."

"Agreed." But clearly Vik had no problem believing his children would be as dedicated to AIH as he was.

Who knew? Maddie herself might have wanted a career in AIH, at least in some capacity, if she'd had a different relationship with her father.

"I think we will have to accept that our children will be influenced by both of us," she told him.

"I can think of much worse things."

"I'm glad you said so," she replied cheekily, secretly touched by his sincerity.

"Open the box," Vik instructed.

"Are you done making promises?"

"Any other commitment I make to you would fall under the three I've already made."

"Three?"

"Fidelity. Dedication. Family."

Inexplicable emotion clogged her throat, but he was right. He'd promised the things that mattered most to her. With a few words he'd committed to building a *family* with her and all that entailed.

She took the lid off the box, incapable of hiding the way her fingers trembled.

Inside, nestled in a bed of black silk, were two rings. One she recognized as a traditionally inspired Russian three-strand wedding band.

Each diamond-encrusted ring interwoven with the others was a different shade of gold: yellow, white and rose.

It was beautiful, but not ostentatious. Perfect for her. Beside it rested a diamond engagement ring set in the pink-tinted gold that would sit flush against the curved wedding band when he put it on her hand.

She didn't ask how he knew the rose tint that used to be known as Russian gold was her favorite. Vik was scary like that.

She didn't ask if she would be able to wear the ring beside the wedding ring after they were married. She could see the curve in the band that would make that possible.

He'd melded the traditions of his homeland with that of his grandparents and taken her own preferences into consideration. It was so Vik. She might not still be in love with him, but it was no wonder she'd never been able to accept a substitute.

"It's beautiful," she breathed, the moment feeling unexpectedly profound.

"As is the woman it was designed for."

"You didn't have this designed for me." He couldn't possibly have.

This kind of custom work wasn't done in a few hours.

He cupped her hands with his own. "You will have to accept that my plans for the future have included you for much longer than you considered me in the same regard."

"I sincerely doubt that." He'd been *it* for her since she'd had her first real thought about boys and girls and how their lives came together.

Even when she hadn't realized she was still comparing every man to Viktor Beck. Darn Romi being right all these years anyway.

He shook his head. "You had a schoolgirl crush, but have not thought of me in that way for six years."

So, he *wasn't* all-knowing. "That shows how much you know. Romi always says I hold other men up to your example and they pale in comparison."

"And what do you say?"

"I always denied it."

"See, I told you."

"I've begun to realize she might have been right." No other man had a chance with Maddie.

Not Perry, not anyone.

Vik's expression dismissed her words as an exaggeration.

"I never forgot you." He'd been too deeply embedded in her psyche, if not her heart.

Maddie had honestly believed her issues with trust had prevented intimacy with another man, but now realized memories of *that guy* had been enough to keep others at bay.

"You avoided me like the plague."

"You did your own avoidance."

"For about a year," he acknowledged. "I missed our friendship. I thought enough time had passed that we'd gotten past the awkward incident."

And he'd approached her. She'd rebuffed him, doing her best to never be put in a position where they could speak privately again. She'd stopped coming home unless her father demanded her attendance and that happened rarely enough.

For at least two years, Maddie had turned down every invite that might put her and Vik in the same sphere.

"I wasn't on the same page." What had been awkward for him had been humiliating for her.

"You made that unmistakable."

"I was angry with you." She'd felt betrayed.

Perry's treachery hurt; Vik's rejection had devastated her.

"And now?" Vik asked.

What did he want her to say? She'd stopped avoiding him at social functions before she graduated from university, but she'd still made sure there was no opportunity for them to renew the old friendship.

"The world looks like a different place from twenty-four than eighteen." It was the best she could do.

"You will forgive me for hurting you?" he asked, like it really mattered.

So, she told him the truth. "I forgave you a long time ago, Vik."

"It did not feel like it."

She looked up into his espresso-brown eyes. "Do you forgive me?"

"For kissing me?" he asked, sounding genuinely confused.

Not a usual circumstance for him. She would take a moment to savor it and even tease him if the discussion wasn't so important.

She explained, "For mistaking your kindness for something more and making our friendship impossible."

"I never held it against you." His tone implied something else altogether.

"You thought you should have known I was falling in love with you," she realized.

"That wasn't the way I termed it, but yes."

Right. He'd thought her love was a crush. But if it had been only a crush, it would have taken months, not years, to get over.

"You're not omniscient, Vik."

"If I'd been paying better attention, I could have headed you off gently."

She wasn't sure that was true. Vik was right that she and her father shared a stubbornness that resulted in a tenacity of purpose almost impossible to derail.

"If we'd remained friends, Perry would never have gotten the hold on you he did."

"You think you would have stopped us becoming friends."

"I would have prevented him from using you as his personal bank and he would have known that you had people looking out for you."

"People scary enough to abandon his plans for the phony exposé before he ever put feelers out for the first reporter?" she asked with a smile.

"You think I'm scary."

"To men like Perry? Oh, yes, definitely."

"But not to you."

"No, Vik, you don't scare me."

"Good."

He frowned. "Perhaps you would not have taken the chances you have in the past years if you'd had the stability of my presence in your life."

"You're pretty arrogant."

"Do you deny it?"

"Actually yes," she said firmly. "My actions are not your fault, or your responsibility."

He shrugged, clearly disagreeing.

"You really have a God complex."

"No, but I know my responsibilities."

"And I'm one of them?" she demanded, frustrated more with herself for seeing that as romantic than Vik for his arrogance.

His smile sent heat through her, reminding her of that lack-of-celibacy thing he'd taken pains to make clear. "I hope more than that."

"Friends again?"

"Yes, definitely."

"But you want more." Maybe not passionately and personally, though she was beginning to see that Vik *did* desire her, but to make his dreams come true, Vik was going to marry her.

"Yes."

"Okay."

"To?"

"Everything."

His expression turned even more heated and predatory. "Be careful what you promise."

"This is a special place. Promises made here stick, right?"

"Yes." No doubts.

"Then I promise to do my best to make both our dreams come true."

"I make this promise as well."

That was way better than him promising to build AIH into some world superpower, in her opinion. "Thank you."

His kiss took her by surprise. It shouldn't have. Wasn't it natural to kiss to seal an engagement?

But the kiss did surprise her. And then it overwhelmed her, his lips coaxing a response that radiated throughout her body. They took possession of hers, no longer coaxing, but insisting on the two things she'd said only that morning she wasn't capable of.

Submission and trust.

But then, like with so many other things in her life, the rules did not apply to Viktor Beck.

She found herself melting into him, no thoughts for self-preservation or holding anything back.

And he accepted her surrender with a forceful masculine desire that belied any claim for a lack of passion between them.

He devoured her mouth, his arms coming around her, his hands pressing her body against his, one thigh pressing between her legs as far as her skirt would allow.

Maddie's knees would have given out, but Vik's hold on her was too tight.

She'd thought the kiss this morning had been hot, but it was nothing like Viktor Beck staking claim to the woman who promised to marry him and give him his dreams.

Viktor knocked impatiently on Madison's door thirty minutes before they needed to be at Jeremy's ostentatious home in Presidio Heights.

Viktor had not given himself time for a drink or idle chitchat on purpose. After the kiss at the overlook, he did not want to risk his self-control before the dinner.

If his grandparents weren't going to be there, as well as the photographer from the magazine, he would never have left Madison that afternoon. But she deserved to show up to her engagement dinner on time and *not* looking like she'd spent the hours before in bed.

He'd told her the truth earlier. Six years ago he'd seen her as barely a woman when she'd kissed him.

He'd been shocked by his own body's response to her overtures, realizing for the first time that she was an adult and *not* a child. Not that he'd given that revelation much credence.

Not at first, but after a year of avoiding her and indulging in more liaisons than his workaholic regime usually allowed for, two things had become obvious.

He missed Madison and she was the only woman he wanted sharing his bed. She was still too young and Viktor's plans didn't include marriage for at least a few more years.

Anything else with the daughter of AIH's president and owner was out of the question. And not just because Viktor considered the older, driven businessman a friend.

Viktor wasn't sure when he realized his own business ambitions included marrying Madison, but it was well before he broached the subject in any oblique way with Jeremy. The older man's concern regarding what would happen when Madison inherited full control of the trust gave Viktor the traction he needed for Jeremy's approval of his own future plans.

He'd had the rings commissioned and intended to launch his courtship of Madison in the coming weeks when Timwater sent a spanner into the works with his "breakup interview."

If Viktor had started his pursuit of Madison earlier, the opportunistic man would not have had a chance to hurt her with his lies. It was unacceptable bad timing that had left Madison vulnerable.

It angered him. Viktor did not do bad timing. And he did not get caught by surprise. But he had not anticipated Timwater's betrayal of his long-standing friendship with the heiress.

While it had not precipitated long-term action on Viktor's part that he wasn't already planning, the intolerable situation had brought things to a head before he intended. *And* it had forced him to work around Jeremy's knee-jerk response to his daughter's misadventure.

While that might have ended up working in Viktor's favor, it had come with additional emotional cost to Madison.

He might be ruthless, but that was not okay with him. Her well-being was his responsibility now.

The door opened and Viktor's thoughts scattered.

Madison's copper curls flirted around her face, her blue eyes vibrant and flashing with a response to his presence that found a corresponding reaction in his body.

Lips entirely too kissable despite the dark color staining them in a perfect scarlet bow curved in a smile of welcome. "Hi, Vik. Are you coming in?"

She'd encased her tempting body in a 1950s-inspired couture cocktail dress in a shiny dark blue that rustled as she moved.

The skirt was full, nipping in at the waist, and the bodice fitted, the artistically cut neckline dipping to reveal the hint of cleavage he found more sexually alluring than any woman he'd seen in a dress that revealed most of her breasts.

"You…" He cleared his throat, finding it unaccountably dry. "You look beautiful."

Only after he spoke did it occur to him that he had not answered her question.

"Thank you." She blushed, something she rarely did anymore. "It works?" The nerves that slipped in to tinge her smile were something else she didn't show others. "Only I wanted your grandparents to see *me,* not the…"

She didn't have to finish. "It will be all right.

Deda and *Babulya* are eager to see you and welcome you into our family."

"They know we are engaged? Have they seen the articles?"

Ignoring his own best intentions, he pushed into the apartment and right into Madison's personal space.

She gasped and looked up at him, eyes wide, breath hitching. "Vik? What?"

He curved his hands around her waist, enjoying the soft slide of the fabric and the heat of her skin under it even more. "They know we are engaged and they are delighted."

"Oh."

"They know about the stories and they are furious with Timwater."

"They don't believe them? You told them he lied, didn't you?"

"I did and they don't." Viktor reveled in the implicit trust in his ability to make things right that could be read into her questions.

"Thank you."

Mindful of the crimson color on her lips, he bent down and pressed a soft kiss to the side of her neck, staying to inhale the subtle fragrance of honeysuckle mixed with orange and a hint of vanilla and her own unique scent. "You smell good."

"It's my perfume."

"It's you. Rosewater would smell just as delicious against your skin."

She trembled against him, her hands pressing into his chest. "Vik."

That was all she said. Just his name. But it was a plea, whether to step back or to do something about the electricity arcing between them, he did not let himself contemplate.

He stepped back. "We need to go. Everyone is waiting."

"Including the photographer."

"He has his instructions to be as unobtrusive as possible."

Madison grimaced, her opinion of how unobtrusive that could actually be very clear.

He looked around and spied her coat over the back of an armchair. Viktor had always enjoyed Madison's efficiency and was glad to see that she had not developed the habit of keeping a man waiting that he always found more irritating than intriguing.

Grabbing the coat, he offered it to her. "We need to head out."

"You cut it a little close." But she didn't hesitate to let him help her into the fitted wool trench coat the same crimson red as her lips.

He saw no reason to hide the truth. "Protecting us both from how much I want you."

"What are you talking about?" she asked,

sounding genuinely confused as she did up the oversized black buttons and tied the belt on her coat.

"You must realize the prospect of having you in my bed has my libido in overdrive." The truth of that was never more blatant to him than in how hard he found it to lead her out of the apartment without once mussing the color of her lipstick.

However, nothing said he had to curb his desire to touch her completely. They made their way to the elevators with his arm around her waist.

"But why would it?" Could she sound more innocent?

He didn't think so.

"You are an incredibly beautiful woman." But more importantly, she was the one woman who sparked desire hot enough to do his ancestors proud.

"You didn't want me before."

"We discussed this. You were barely more than a child." And he *had* wanted her.

"You're right," she said distractedly. "But—"

"Nothing. Trust me. I want you. Six years ago, the timing was wrong, but I will gladly offer you all the proof you desire later tonight, *after* dinner with our respective families."

"You want to come back to my apartment tonight?" she squeaked, charming him.

The elevator doors closed, giving a false sense

of privacy he had to once again fight taking advantage of.

"You have no reason to be nervous," he assured her. "I am not an animal in the bedroom."

Even if he wanted her with heretofore untapped primal mating instincts.

"Vik…" She blinked up at him, her lips parted slightly. "I told you, I'm a virgin."

"What?" The elevator doors opened but he didn't step out, his brain short-circuiting.

"I told you—"

"That you hadn't been in a serious relationship." But that didn't mean she hadn't had sex. Things happened. She was twenty-four. This was not possible.

"No random hookups."

"Ever?" he asked in disbelief.

"I told you I had no experience."

"In BDSM."

"In anything."

"That will change." Viktor was not above using whatever means necessary to ensure the future he planned. Including being Madison's first lover.

The fact he wanted her more than any woman he had ever known was beside the point.

She stepped off the elevator into the parking garage. "I don't think being engaged to you is going to be anything like I was imagining."

"If you thought it was going to be without sexual intimacy, I'd have to say you are right," he said as he helped her buckle into the passenger seat of his car.

He gave in to the urge that had been riding him since the moment she'd opened her door and kissed her. He reined in his desire. Barely. And stepped back.

He closed her door and took several deep breaths before moving around the car to slide into the driver's seat.

Her eyes glowing with blue fire, she asked, "No pretense of waiting for our wedding night?"

"We made our vows at the overlook this afternoon. Nothing said later between us will be any more profound." He started the engine, but didn't back out of the parking spot, waiting with an odd feeling in his chest for her reply.

"I thought it felt that way…like it was profound."

"It was." He put the car in gear.

"So what? You consider us married now?" She sounded like she didn't believe her own words and yet he knew she had felt the weight of the promises they'd made earlier.

"As good as, yes."

"You make your own rules, don't you?"

"You are just now figuring this out?"

CHAPTER SEVEN

THE ENGAGEMENT DINNER was a lot more enjoyable than Maddie had expected it to be.

Especially considering the fact the guest list had grown to include some Archer second cousins, a Madison great-aunt, one of Misha's nephews and his wife, who just happened to be visiting friends who owned a vineyard outside of Napa, and Romi.

Maddie's father was all smiles, though underlying his bonhomie was an unfamiliar reticence with her that gave Maddie a certain level of comfort. He had not escaped this morning's debacle in the conference room unscathed.

Small winces indicated he did not like her new habit of calling him by his first name, either, but if he wanted her to stop, he'd have to ask. Nicely. And behave like a father. Somehow.

She hadn't started calling him Jeremy to hurt him, but because it simply hurt *her* too much to refer to a man who treated her like a stranger more often than not as Father.

Vik acted as a buffer between them, not exactly a new role for him, but one he hadn't played with any consistency in six years.

Taking it a step further than he used to, Vik actually physically stood between her and others in unconscious protection whenever she felt herself growing uneasy. While no one had the bad taste to actually mention the articles spawned by Perry's lies, family could manage intrusiveness in subtle ways strangers never could.

Thankfully, Vik seemed to recognize her moods—sometimes even before she did—and took steps to make sure the questions didn't get a chance to edge into being blatantly intrusive.

Tellingly, no one seemed to find it hard to believe they'd been carrying on a relationship outside the media's radar for months now. Not even Misha's nephew evinced surprise at the engagement.

Everyone was happy to congratulate Maddie and Vik, making her feel like maybe this thing could really work.

Regardless of what had precipitated the engagement, their friends and family considered them a good match. A big part of her agreed.

She only hoped she wasn't making a huge mistake…that Vik was the man she was discovering. More the white knight in Armani than the heartless tycoon following in her father's footsteps that she'd seen him as for the past six years.

Vik's grandparents were wonderful, as always.

Misha was a gray-haired, slightly stooped version of Vik with an exuberant warmth very unlike his more reserved grandson. A retired scientist, Ana was both highly intelligent and gently affectionate by nature. She wasn't as overt as her husband, but she would make a wonderful great-grandmother for Maddie and Vik's children.

The magazine photographer turned out to be extremely good at fading into the background and Maddie found herself relaxing and enjoying the first real family dinner she remembered since her mother's death.

"Your grandparents are such nice people." Maddie allowed Vik to remove her coat and his own before taking both of them and hanging them in the hall closet.

Such a simple thing to do. She'd done it hundreds of times for other guests, but never with the same homey feeling—or sense of irrevocability that washed over her as she closed the closet door.

Vik was staying the night.

And Maddie's heart was pounding in her chest like a bass drum.

Not from fear, though. No, nothing like it, though that surprised her. Shouldn't there be at least a little anxiety?

She'd never done this before, after all.

But all she felt was excitement.

Maybe it was because she knew Vik would leave if she asked him to. Only she didn't want him to leave.

She wanted him to follow through on the promise of passion in their kisses earlier. Besides, if they weren't compatible in bed, that could be a real problem.

Right?

Only what were the chances when his kisses turned her inside out. Self-justification much?

She made a sound of self-deprecating humor.

"Liking my family is a source of amusement for you?" Vik's hands landed on her shoulders before he turned her to face him.

His expression wasn't mocking or judging, just inquisitive.

She smiled up at the beloved handsome face as she shook her head. "No, I was thinking about the things we tell ourselves to justify doing what we want to do."

His look promised things she'd never experienced but was pretty darn sure she wanted to. "What *things* do you want to do?"

"Like you don't know."

He shook his head. "I'm still a little stunned you've never done them before."

"Pretty pathetic, huh?"

"In what way were you pathetic?" Vik asked in a tone that didn't bode well for anyone who might have used that word to describe her.

Including herself.

She liked the feelings his instant protectiveness engendered in her despite the fact she thrived on her independence.

Feeling a little odd about that, she moved away from him and crossed the living room, which was decorated in her favorite shabby chic. While she loved the perfect blend of distressed wood furniture, floral damasks, lifelike silk bouquets set in epoxy to look like water, the pristine whites and abundance of feminine styling screamed "single woman living alone" to her.

And while there was *nothing* bad about that, she wasn't as pleased by the fact she'd never even had a short-term relationship. She'd be happier if something in her home indicated the need to take someone else's preferences, or even needs, into account.

"What would you call a twenty-four-year-old virgin?" she asked, turning back to face him.

"Picky." His smile melted her.

She grinned up at him. "That's one word for it."

"You were waiting for me." She could tell by his tone he thought he was joking.

A sudden revelation hit her. Romi had definitely been right all along. "I was."

She might have been able to get over her first love, but Maddie had never moved on from thinking that Viktor Beck would be the ideal lover. And so she had turned down every other man.

Yes, trust was an issue for her, but right along with her lack of trust in other men had been a primal certainty of whom she wanted to share her body with.

A certainty she'd been consciously denying but living under for the past six years.

Espresso eyes darkened with unmistakable lust, blowing her mind. He wanted her. He'd said he did. He'd kissed her like he did, but that look?

It was imbued with the same primitive passion she'd acknowledged in herself. So predatory. It sent shivers chasing along her nerve endings.

"You were made for me," he said, confirming it wasn't her imagination.

The driving force between them was very mutual.

"A pity you didn't realize that six years ago." She regretted the words as soon as she said them and shook her head. "Forget I said that."

Maddie got why Vik had turned her down before. Wishing they'd already taken this step so she wouldn't be dealing with her public humiliation right now was both futile and borderline ridiculous. Because even if they'd gotten together then, there was no guarantee they would still be together now.

His jaw firm, his lips set in a determined line, Vik moved toward her with intent. "I was not ready for marriage and you were not ready for me."

"I—"

His finger pressing against her lips stopped the argument. "We both had living to do."

"You were really thinking about *this* then?" she asked with surprise she couldn't hide.

"Yes."

"But you weren't happy about it." Wasn't happy about the memory if his current expression was anything to go by.

"You were eighteen. I was still used to thinking of you as a child. It felt wrong."

"I was an adult, a grown woman." But even as she made the claim, she knew that compared to Vik she *had* been a child.

"You could vote, join the armed forces and take on your own debt. That didn't mean you were ready for a relationship with a man like me."

"A relationship, or sex?"

"Same thing when it comes to you and me."

"Is it?"

"It has always been marriage or nothing between us, Madison." Vik reached out and traced the line of her bodice, his fingertip never straying from the sapphire-blue taffeta of her dress to the skin of her bosom.

Her breath hitched, but she didn't move away. "Because of AIH."

"Because my grandfather raised me to be a man with a sense of honor." The "unlike Frank Beck" went unsaid, but she heard it anyway.

Vik would never be like the father that had caused both him and his grandparents so much grief and disappointment.

"You may be a shark, Vik, but you're an honest one."

He smiled wryly, his fingertip resting on the point of the V dipping between her breasts. "And I don't eat guppies for breakfast."

"Am I a guppy?" she asked breathlessly.

"No." Satisfaction burned in his dark gaze. "You are a twenty-four-year-old woman."

The emphasis he placed on the word *woman* was a conversation all in itself.

"You planned to marry me before Perrygate ever happened."

"I did." Vik looked with significance down at the custom ring on her finger and she caught on.

There was no denying the truth in front of

her eyes. "You really did have the rings made for me."

"I do not lie."

"No, but…" The scope of what he was saying left her grasping for words that would not come.

"Timwater forced me to move my plans forward, but only by a couple of weeks."

"You were going to ask me to marry you?"

"I planned to date you first," he said with some wry humor, almost self-deprecatingly. "We needed to rebuild the rapport we once had."

His thinking made him a different man than her father in ways she didn't feel like enumerating, but wouldn't deny. "You recognized before Jeremy did that the only way my father would have an heir to leave in charge of the business is if I married him."

"Yes."

"So, you made plans to play on my father's desire to leave his legacy to *family*." It was brilliant. And manipulative.

But he'd already shown that as important as his own plans for AIH were to Vik, he would not ignore Maddie's happiness. He'd offered to buy her a building for her dream as a wedding gift.

Calculated? Maybe, but *for* her benefit, not to her detriment.

Vik's silence was answer enough. Not only

had he strategized, but he'd also started working on her father already. Jeremy had come to the whole "his daughter must marry to save herself and the company's reputation" pretty darn quickly otherwise.

"I'm not sure how I feel about this," she admitted.

She understood. To an extent.

But it still felt like she'd been maneuvered.

Vik's touch finally strayed entirely from her dress to the upper swell of her breasts, tracing the same path as before, only along her skin this time. "While you are deciding, take into account that if you had been a different woman, my plans would have taken a different direction."

She shivered, her breath quavering in her chest until another thought came to her. "You would have taken AIH out from under my father?"

Horrified because as much as she didn't get her father, she loved him, and she was certain Vik would have done exactly that. Rather than allow a stranger to come in and take over what he considered to be his.

Vik shrugged, neither confirming, nor denying. "It was not necessary."

"You said Jeremy is your friend."

"He is."

"But you would still take his company."

"I would not have betrayed him."

No. That wasn't Vik's style. "You still would have figured out a way."

"Does that upset you?"

"I said before that you're ruthless."

"This is not news."

No, it really wasn't. "My mind doesn't work like yours."

"Make no mistake, you have your own brand of ruthlessness, but if you were too much like me, we would not fit so well together." Both his hands moved to settle on her waist.

She was distracted by the sensation of his thumbs brushing up and down against her lower ribs. "You think we fit?"

"I know we do."

"So, you're saying you don't just want the company. You want me, too." Not just sex with her, but Maddie as a complete person.

At least the Madison Archer he knew about. What would Vik think of Maddie Grace?

"You will support my dreams in a way a woman of less strength could not do."

"Your plans would have been really messed up if I'd picked one of the other candidates Jeremy put forward." She gave in to the irresistible urge to poke at the bear.

Vik's gorgeous mouth twisted in disdain. "You were never going to choose another man."

"You don't think so?"

"I know."

"Another word for excessive confidence is arrogance."

"I prefer honest."

She laughed softly and then had a revelation. "You manipulated the choice of candidates."

"I was not expecting Maxwell Black."

"Neither was I." And she still wanted to know what the man had done to Romi. "He's intense."

"He's a good businessman."

"Is he honorable?"

"Yes."

"As honorable as you?"

Vik considered his answer for a second. "I would do business with him on a handshake."

"Good to know."

"Why? Considering your options?" He didn't sound too worried by the prospect.

"According to you, there are no other options."

"True." Vik looked like he was considering what he was going to say next. "We grew up together."

"What? Like in the same neighborhood?"

"Same Russian-American-dominated street, same school, same afternoons spent in activities sponsored by the Russian cultural center."

"Were you friends?"

"We still are...of a sort."

"You're too alike to be really close."

"We jockeyed for the top place in class until we went to different universities."

"No one else had a chance."

"No."

Maddie bit her lip, but finally decided she would be honest about her concerns. "Romi dated him."

Vik's gaze flared. "I see."

"He's intense," Maddie repeated.

"Are they still dating?"

"No."

"Then..."

"I don't need to be worried?"

"He is a good man."

When it was Viktor Beck making the claim, Maddie believed him.

"Are you really spending the night?" she asked, focusing on what mattered most in the present moment.

"Yes."

"After a single day." One day in which they had decided to get married, made that decision public and negotiated a future they could both live with.

"In one respect, but between us?" He pulled her body close so they shared heat. "Tonight is the culmination of ten years."

"We've barely spoken in six."

"When was the last time Frank was in town?" Vik asked her, like she'd know.

And she did. "Three months ago. He was in San Francisco for Christmas." Vik's father had attended Jeremy's holiday party along with Misha and Ana.

Vik nodded, his expression dour. "*Babulya* was pleased."

"But you couldn't wait for him to leave."

"You are the only person who knew that."

She found that hard to believe, but then… maybe not. Vik didn't wear his emotions on his sleeve.

But that wasn't the point, was it? "Just because I saw your father at my father's home and knew he was in town doesn't mean you and I communicated in any meaningful way."

"Didn't we?"

Okay, so in the past two years, they'd had increasing numbers and depths of conversations. And it struck her. She'd thought she was just being grown-up about the past, but he'd been working on rebuilding that rapport he had mentioned earlier.

The man made Machiavelli look like a preschooler in the art of the deep play.

"Still." Not a brilliant comeback, but what she had.

Vik smiled that shark's smile. "When was the last time I took a date to an event?"

So, she knew the answer. She'd revealed earlier in the car with Conrad how closely she watched Vik without meaning to watch him at all. "That doesn't mean anything."

"Doesn't it?"

"Vik…"

"I believe both the fact that I have not had another woman on my arm in over a year *and the fact you know that* is significant."

"Really?" she drawled sarcastically even as she couldn't help wondering if he was right.

"I know that you haven't dated, either. I wasn't entirely sure about Timwater, but the way you two are together doesn't imply sexual intimacy."

"I should hope not."

"Besides, he was sleeping with other women."

She'd suspected, though Perry had always tried to play it like he didn't sleep around. She wasn't sure why. It wouldn't have mattered to her either way.

Vik knowing however, meant he'd been paying attention. "You have a file on him, don't you?"

"Naturally."

"And Romi?"

"Romi has been your friend for longer than me."

"You're saying you don't have a file."

Vik leaned down and spoke softly, right into Maddie's ear. "I'm saying I don't need one."

It wasn't exactly sweet nothings, but she still shivered from the sensation of his breath gently blowing across her ear.

"You know her well, too," Maddie said, not even sure why she was trying to keep the conversation going.

"Yes."

Curiosity and concern prompted her to ask, "Did you know she'd dated Maxwell?"

"No."

"Good. I don't feel like I was so oblivious."

Vik straightened, but didn't move back. "I'm sure if you did not know, they both took pains to keep it private."

"You're right." While Maddie was still worried, she didn't feel like a bad friend anymore.

She let herself fall into his deep coffee gaze, even as she relaxed more completely into his body. "I want to kiss you."

Bad friend, or good one, Maddie didn't want to think about anyone except her and Vik right now.

"What is stopping you?" He leaned down so their lips were a fraction of an inch apart, taking away the only barrier that mattered.

She moved toward him, speaking in a breath against his lips. "Nothing."

The first brush of her lips against his electrified her. It was the barest of caresses, but near unbearable in its intimacy. She was staking a claim with the featherlight touch and he was accepting that claim as surely as she'd accepted his promises earlier.

They were distinctly different, one set of lips masculine, the other feminine, and yet they fit with the perfection of molds aligned and cast simultaneously.

Vik's response was full-on alpha man, accepting her mouth with his and then turning it around and moving his lips against hers, driving the kiss to greater sensation and closeness.

Nipping oh-so-gently with his teeth on her lower lip, he demanded entrance. With no thought but to give it, she let her lips fall open.

His tongue swept into her mouth and just that fast Maddie was drowning in a sexual response only this man had ever brought out in her, thoughts and emotions overwhelmed by the onslaught of devastating sensuality.

Vik's hold on her tightened as he pulled her body completely flush with his, his big hands roving over her back and up to knead her scalp.

Her own hands slid of their own volition up his pecs, over his shoulders and to the back of his neck, pulling her body around so her breasts were crushed against his chest. Sparks of delicious sensation pricked her nipples nearly to the point of pain in their intensity.

It felt so incredible still dressed, she could not fathom what it would be like once they were naked skin pressed to naked skin.

Vik made a rumbling sound of approval in his throat before his body shifted and then she was being lifted into his arms as he stood.

The man was strong. Following on that thought came another.

They were really going to do this.

For the first time, Maddie was glad she was a twenty-four-year-old virgin.

She wanted no past experiences shadowing this moment with him. No memories of hands on her flesh but his.

Vik carried her unerringly into to her bedroom, lowering her back to her feet and pulling his mouth from hers. She didn't want to stop and used her hold on his neck to lift herself back up so the kiss could continue.

It was only natural to swing her legs up and around his waist, locking her ankles behind his back.

Something about her actions flipped a switch in Vik and the kiss went nuclear. His mouth devoured hers as he cupped her bottom through the rustling silk of her dress's full skirt.

Overwhelmed by sensation, Maddie lost her connection to anything but the kiss. She did not know how long their mouths ate at each other.

Nothing registered but the sparks of pleasure he ignited in her rapidly fanning into a conflagration that consumed.

She wasn't even aware he'd moved them to the bed until he broke away from her and she didn't fall to the floor.

She mewled with her need to reconnect to his lips, a sound that would have mortified her if she was not too lost to desire to care.

"Vik!" she demanded, no other word coming to the forefront of her mind.

His smile was feral and hot. But the wink that came with it was hotter. "Clothes."

CHAPTER EIGHT

ONE WORD BUT it was all Maddie needed.

She sat up and reached back to unzip her dress. It was tricky at the best of times, the top of the zipper hitting her in the center of her back.

With her hands trembling from need, it was impossible. So frustrated she could almost cry, she struggled to unzip it.

All the while, she couldn't pull her eyes from Vik. He'd ripped his Armani sweater off and tossed it on the floor, the black T-shirt he wore under it joining the pile of cashmere a second later.

His belt made a whoosh as he pulled it out of his trousers and the buckle clunked against the wall when he tossed it. His tailored slacks were next, dropping to reveal a straining bulge behind dark designer briefs.

"Your body is beautiful," she breathed in awe.

Every muscle of his six-foot-four-inch frame was honed. Dark hair covered his chest, narrowing to a trail that disappeared into the waistband of his briefs.

She didn't know if it was the dark, clingy fabric or reality, or even her oversensitized emotions, but Vik looked huge.

Maddie's thighs clenched even as her fingers itched to touch. And she hadn't seen the actual package yet.

Vik looked back, his own expression filled with desire. "You're still dressed," he accused.

"I know," she said with pure frustration.

He winked again, the expression just as mind-bogglingly sexy this time as the first. "Need some help there?"

"Yes."

He stalked toward the bed like a big sleek cat, climbing on with the same grace. He reached around her and let his fingers trail down the shallow V of her dress to the top of the zipper. "Is this your problem?"

"I can't reach it."

"How did you get dressed then?"

"I wasn't hampered then."

"By what?"

"What do you think?" she asked, wanting to sound annoyed and only succeeding in revealing the need inside her.

"Me?"

"Desire," she clarified.

"Desire for me."

"Yes," she admitted, no real reason to pretend otherwise, but annoyed all the same at having to say it out loud.

"Good." He lowered the zipper inch by inch. "I like this dress."

"I'm never wearing it again."

"Please do."

"Why?"

"I have always enjoyed unwrapping my gifts. Just ask my grandparents."

"I'm not a Christmas package."

"No, you are something far more valuable." He kissed the corner of her mouth and then brushed her lips with his lightly. "You are the woman who will share my life."

"You're awfully good at romance for a corporate shark."

He wasn't kidding about enjoying the process of unwrapping. Time moved by in increments measured by her rising passion as he took off first her dress, removing it to reveal her body one slow inch at a time. His desire-filled gaze burned her with sensual appreciation.

The silk foundations she wore under the dress came next, but he took even more time with those than the blue taffeta, kissing bits of her flesh as it was revealed, sensitizing her body in ways she'd no idea he could do.

When he was done, she was a naked, quivering mass of sexual need.

And he still had his briefs on.

She tugged at the waistband, her voice husky with passion when she managed to force the words past the tightness in her throat. "Take them off."

"Not yet."

"Why?" she demanded, patience in another universe.

"You are a virgin."

"So?" He was going to change that, wasn't he?

"So, you need preparation and I'm on a hair trigger where you are concerned."

"You have to take your underwear off to make love to me," she spelled out slowly, like she wasn't sure he got it.

He bared his teeth in a smile that had no humor. "And before that happens I will make sure you are ready to receive me."

"But—"

"You will have to trust me on this." His eyes demanded her acquiescence.

She didn't know if she could give it. "I want you!"

"And you will have me."

Vik's hand slipped between her legs right then, fingers delving in the moist heat no other man had ever touched, and she cried out. He touched her in ways she'd only ever dreamed of being touched, caressed her to her first shattering climax before she even realized what that desperate feeling inside her was leading to.

She'd touched herself, but it had never felt like this. She was still trembling with spent pleasure when a single long masculine finger slipped inside her. Something shifted in her heart at the intimate intrusion.

He was not inside her, not the way she'd always imagined, but they were connected on a level that corresponded to a place inside her soul.

He pressed upward and she winced with pain.

"Hurt?" he asked, his own tone strained.

"A little."

"It will sting."

"Why?"

"I am going to break your hymen with my finger. It will make the actual penetration of my sex easier on you." The words were clinical, but his tone and the concern in his expression was not.

He'd thought this through and that touched her in the same place in her soul his intimate intrusion had.

He pressed a little harder.

A sharp shard of pain stabbed her. "It more than stings!"

"I am sorry." He grimaced. "It will be worth it."

She wasn't so sure about that, but trusted him enough to give him the benefit of the doubt.

That trust was sorely tested a moment later when the pain increased to the point that she felt like he was invading her with a hot poker, not his finger. She gasped and tried to pull away, surprised when she succeeded in dislodging his hand.

He leaned back on his haunches, the telltale traces of blood on his finger a testament to his success.

Grateful that the pain was already morphing to a low-level throbbing rather than stabbing, she asked, "Now?"

"Not yet. There is more to do."

The more included him stripping naked finally. In the bathroom, where he ran a very hot bath.

He looked even bigger jutting out from his body than he had with his erection tucked behind black silk knit.

He smiled at her with gentle humor. "Your eyes are as wide as saucers."

"You're as big as a baseball bat."

That startled a laugh out of him. "Not even close."

"Right."

"Your eyes are playing tricks on you."

Unsure where it came from, annoyance drove

her stomping across the tiled floor and gave her the boldness to grope him in her fist. "My fingers are not touching."

The sound he made was not a word.

Viscous drops formed on the tip of the flesh in her hand. She touched it with her fingertip and brought it to her mouth, licking it cautiously.

Surprisingly it was almost sweet, with only a hint of the salty bitterness she'd heard about. "I like it."

He groaned and then jerked his body backward so his hard flesh slipped from her hand. "Bath. Now."

"Why?"

"Can't you just trust me?"

"I trust you more than any other man on this planet." He might be the only man on the planet she *did* trust. He had to know that.

"It will make it better for you," he explained.

"How do you know?" she demanded. "Have you had sex with many virgins?"

She found that possibility seriously disturbing.

"None," he practically snarled as he lifted her up and set her in the bathtub with surprisingly gentle movements, considering his apparent irritation. "I read up on it."

"Because you're a planner."

"Yes." He still sounded like a man ready to take someone's head off.

"Why are you mad?" she asked plaintively.

"I'm not angry!"

"You're snarling at me."

"I'm turned on." The low growl rumbled through her.

"So am I. The bath was your idea!"

"For your benefit."

Oh, man. "I'm sorry. This isn't easy for you, is it?"

"Waiting?" He stepped into the bath behind her, pulling her into his lap, his hands settling on her possessively. "No, my sexy little redhead, it is not easy, but you are worth it."

Another white-knight moment. "If you aren't careful, you're going to have me believing in fairy tales."

His only answer was one languid touch to her thigh. That caress was followed by another and another and another, all over her body and each touch accompanied by the ever-present presence of his hardness pressed against the small of her back.

Her nipples were aching and sensitive, her clitoris vibrating with pleasure, and her entire body melted over his by the time his hands stilled their insidious movements.

There were no words left in her brain when he drained the tub and lifted her back to the tile floor. They dried off in silence, bodies aware and straining toward each other.

She and Vik stripped the bedding back without acknowledging that was what they were going to do, and then together they fell to the mattress covered by the single sheet.

The lovemaking was everything she had ever dreamed it would be, his sex filling her so deeply she felt like they'd really bonded into one entity in that moment.

There was still some pain, but nothing stabbing and dark, and the pleasure pushed any lingering discomfort to the bottom register of Maddie's awareness.

This time when she climaxed, she screamed until her throat protested the strain. Vik grew impossibly hard inside her, his body going rigid just before he shouted his own release in the form of a single word.

"Mine."

She didn't even think about birth control until the next morning.

Viktor came to awareness in the dark, two things at the forefront of his mind. The woman he'd craved for years was now in his arms and they hadn't used birth control the first time they made love.

The former gave him satisfaction and the latter a twinge of regret. In a perfect world, they would have a couple years of marriage to enjoy their time together as a couple, to solidify their relationship.

In the real world, Madison had been forced into marriage by the actions of that bastard who had called himself her friend, and Viktor's grandparents were getting on in years. If his children were to have the time to enjoy them as Viktor had, they would have to come along sooner than later.

Viktor had taken advantage of Timwater's idiocy. He could deal with the consequences of other realities, too.

For him, family was everything.

It was the reason he'd been driven to succeed. The one thing that drove him most intensely was the desire to not only make his grandparents proud, but to also provide for his own family as his own father had not done.

Viktor had determined early in his life never to walk a single step in his own father's shoes.

When he'd first met Jeremy Archer, Viktor had believed he'd found the mentor he sought. And he had, but he had also come to the realization that as wrapped up in AIH as Jeremy was, his vision was still too limited.

Both in a business sense and when it came to family.

Jeremy had never understood that all of AIH's success meant nothing in the face of his spectacular failure with his daughter.

Madison was Viktor's match in every way. They were not just sexually compatible, they were combustible. Just as he'd known they would be.

But equally important, they were friends with compatible, if very different, goals for the future.

Viktor felt an unfamiliar sense of having dodged a bullet with Maxwell Black's presence in the conference room that morning. Jeremy bringing in Maxwell—of all men—had precipitated actions on Viktor's part he hadn't intended to take until later.

But he couldn't complain about the outcome.

He in no way regretted making love to Madison and had every intention of showing her that no other man would be her match as Viktor was.

He wasn't just the perfect successor for AIH, he was perfect for Madison.

With that thought, he brushed his hand down her flank, leaning over to kiss the side of her neck and bring her to wakefulness for another example of how very well they meshed in bed.

For the first time in her life, Maddie had woken in another person's arms.

She lay, warm and secure as half of Vik's

body covered hers, his breath still even and slow in sleep.

And she thought of babies and the possibility of family. Had he done it on purpose? Or had he been as lost to the final satiation of years' worth of unfulfilled desire that the idea of birth control hadn't even entered the picture?

Before she'd been made love to by a man who never seemed to get enough, she would have written the latter off as a complete improbability.

But Vik had woken her several times in the night and pushed the boundaries of pleasure and her body on each occasion, his hunger for her something she would never again be able to doubt. There'd been no question when they *were* sleeping that they would do so skin-to-skin.

The one time she'd tried donning her sleep pants and tank top, he'd gotten this look in his eyes. Really intense, feral and determined. Her pajamas had been in a puddle on the floor moments later and her body humming the music of the Viktor Beck pleasure symphony.

Even now, his oversized sex…

No, she didn't believe him that he was no bigger than most men. She'd heard on one of those talk shows hosted by a group of interesting and mostly famous women that the average length was just about five inches erect. Well, she knew from five inches and his was nearly twice that. Average? She did not think so.

Right now, that not-at-all-average hardness was pressing against her hip, telling her that when he woke he'd be ready for more physical intimacy. Despite the twinges of soreness making her aware of muscles she hadn't known she had, nipples that ached from all the stimulation they'd enjoyed and a tender feeling in the flesh between her legs, she knew she wouldn't hesitate to respond.

Except...they hadn't used any form of birth control in the long night of passion. Not once.

"I can hear you thinking." Vik's early morning voice rumbled above her head.

"You said we would make any decision about children together."

Tension seeped into his big body, but he did not move away. "Yes?"

"We did not use birth control last night."

Oddly, he relaxed. "No, we did not."

"Vik," she said in warning.

He sat up, somehow getting pillows propped against the headboard behind him and her sideways in his lap with a minimum of movement. It was a position he apparently enjoyed.

He tilted her chin up, bringing their gazes into alignment. "We made that decision together."

"I didn't make a decision at all. I didn't even think of it."

His eyebrows rose. "Neither did I."

She narrowed her eyes, trying to gauge the truth of his statement. She might be blind, but Maddie couldn't see the smallest flicker of deceit in the espresso orbs.

"It never once occurred to you that a condom might be a good idea?" she asked.

It was his turn for his eyes to narrow, but they glittered with anger not concentration. "You believe I would lie to you?"

"No, but you're ruthless enough to take advantage of an expedient situation."

He agreed, no sign of embarrassment at the truth. "Yes, but to what end would I ignore birth control?"

"You get five percent of the company when I give birth to our first child." Did she really have to remind him of that fact?

"Did you plan to wait to start a family?"

"No." She couldn't even claim not to have thought of it.

Dreams were something even a woman who didn't believe in fairy tales could indulge in. And Maddie's dreams included building the kind of family she'd always wanted to have.

"I did not think you did." Therefore, he had no need to take advantage of circumstance.

"Okay."

"Okay, what?"

"I believe you."

He kissed the tip of her nose. "As you should."

She wrinkled her nose. "It might be old-fashioned, but I would still like to wait until we are married to conceive our first child." Though if she *was* pregnant, she would accept that as the gift she believed it to be.

"Agreed."

"So, from now on, birth control," she insisted.

"Agreed."

"You're being awfully compliant."

"The truth? I would prefer to wait a couple of years before having children."

"Oh." She hadn't considered he wasn't keen on starting a family right away.

"But my grandparents are in their seventies," Vik continued. "If my children are to have the benefit of *Deda* and *Babulya's* presence in their lives, we cannot indulge me."

"I see." Wow.

Once again, she was reminded that while she and Vik might be motivated by different hopes for the future, they both had them. And lucky for her, they dovetailed, as surprising as that might be.

"I hesitate to point this out," Vik said. "Because I *do* want to gift my grandparents with the next generation of our family."

"What?" Maddie couldn't believe how comfortable she was having this discussion naked and sitting in his lap on the bed.

"Won't it be difficult to start your school if we have a baby right away?" he asked.

She gave him a self-deprecating grimace. "I say all the time that money doesn't matter to me, but the truth is, I'm counting on it to be able to 'have it all,' as they say."

"You plan to have a nanny?" He sounded almost shocked.

And she loved him all the more for it. "Probably, but not to *raise* our children. However, if we are ever going to be able to leave the house, we have to have someone besides your grandparents we can trust to care for our children."

"Yes."

"So, we'll have a nanny, someone who fits into our family, preferably matronly in both appearance and age." So, sue her if Maddie didn't want a beautiful young woman living under Vik's nose in their house.

"What do you mean about the money then?"

"I have every intention of hiring qualified staff who share mine and Romi's vision to run the school."

Vik's dark brow furrowed. "But you will both still give a great deal of time to the school. You will have to."

"Yes, but we'll make it work. Romi and I already discussed what would happen in the event one or both of us had a family."

"I'm not surprised."

"My father would be." He'd always assumed she had no business sense if she didn't want to be part of *his* business.

"Jeremy only sees part of the picture when he looks at you," Vik agreed pragmatically.

"That's all he's interested in." Jeremy Archer had never wanted to give the time necessary to get to know who Maddie was, not before Helene's death and definitely not after.

"He *can* break out of his tunnel vision."

"So you say. I've witnessed no evidence."

Vik shook his head, clearly done with the topic. "You'll need an efficient and knowledge-able personal assistant."

"Exactly." A nanny for convenience, not necessity, but a PA? That Maddie would *need* to make sure things got done.

Vik's phone rang before they could continue their discussion. It was Conrad, excited about the opportunity for a live interview with the newly engaged couple on an evening celebrity-news show.

And so it began.

The next weeks passed in a whirl of activity. Interviews as a couple, interviews by herself. The media furor around Maddie and Vik's engagement was even bigger than the initial craziness Perrygate had spawned.

Vik slept at her apartment every night while decorators and contractors worked overtime getting Parean Hall habitable for them. Maddie interviewed domestic staff while overseeing the changes to the main rooms and the master suite. She did her best to make sure both her and Vik's design aesthetic was incorporated in their new home.

And could hear his voice saying "I told you so" when she realized she knew enough about his preferences to do that.

Maddie went back to her secret volunteering in her brown wig and contacts, dressed in clothes from the local superstore. Every minute spent with the children cemented her determination to do more.

She also scheduled a visit with the therapist she'd seen in the immediate months after her skydiving accident, when Maddie had realized the time had come to break away from her past. Dr. MacKenzie was vocal in her praise for how far Maddie had come in dealing with both her mom's death and her father's emotional neglect.

However the therapist evinced some concern about the marriage that Vik said he intended to be *real* and yet was connected to a very lucrative contract for him. Dr. MacKenzie asked Maddie to consider carefully her reasons for agreeing to the engagement.

So Maddie did and, even more importantly, she talked to Vik about it.

"Yes, the contract your father offered is beneficial to me, but getting married right now is important for you, too."

"You think I said yes to the whole marriage thing because of the school, don't you?" Had she?

She'd told herself on that crazy, surrealistic day that was exactly why she needed to consider the idea seriously.

But Vik just shrugged. "Even if the scandal had blown up like it could have, you would not have given up on the school. Romi would have been the public face to run it and you would have been the silent partner as I now will be."

She loved his confidence in her. The pleasure of it masked the full import of his words for a moment, but then it settled in.

"*You* will?" When had Vik offered to partner with her and Romi in founding the school?

"We made promises to see one another's dreams fulfilled. Marriage to you will give me AIH. I've told you that I will ensure it provides for your dreams as well."

Maybe she should have expected something

like this, but she hadn't. "You really are my white knight."

"I thought you did not believe in fairy tales." His voice and expression were teasing, but something told her he liked her claim.

"Maybe I just believe in you." He had always been the exception, the one man she trusted— even when she hadn't thought she had a reason to.

Refusing to admit it didn't make it any less true.

"You do," he said with a mix of implacability and smugness that should have annoyed her.

It didn't. She liked it. "So certain."

"Of you? Yes."

Ultimately, it all came down to that simple truth. *She* trusted Vik to keep the promises he'd made at the Marin Headlands overlook.

The fact that she was falling in love with Viktor Beck all over again? Well, that was something she didn't bring up even to Romi.

How could she help it? The man spent more time masquerading as a white knight than a business tycoon.

The wedding was going forward. And soon.

For the ceremony itself, they planned a very small gathering, but the reception would be huge and attended by the cream of society, the scions of the business world and even a few celebrities.

When Maddie's follow-up therapy appointment conflicted with a meeting with the caterers for their wedding reception, she told Vik she didn't want to reschedule her time with Dr. MacKenzie.

"You are seeing a therapist?" Vik asked. "Why didn't I know this?" The latter clearly the only thing that bothered him about her revelation.

"Because I didn't tell you?"

He made a scoffing sound.

"No one knows except Romi."

"When did you start seeing him?"

"Her. And right after the skydiving incident." Maddie had realized she was taking the same self-destructive path as her mother and she wasn't going to do that. "I saw her weekly for a couple of months and then a few more times after that."

"I'm impressed."

"You are?" She had worried a little he would think she was weak for needing to see someone.

"You realized you couldn't help children if you didn't deal with your own childhood issues."

That had been exactly it. "How do you know me so well?" she asked, falling a little more in love with him right then.

"You know the answer to that."

"You make it a point to get to know everything about the people and businesses you plan to partner with, or take over."

"Our partnership will supersede all others. Of course, I will know everything about you."

She liked hearing that, even if it wasn't exactly true. "But you didn't know I was seeing Dr. MacKenzie."

"No." He sounded chagrined.

Maddie laughed. "Even you are not infallible, Vik."

"Miss Grayson knew."

"She's my best friend."

"What am I?"

"The man I'm going to marry. The man I'm falling in love with all over again." There, she'd said it.

What he did with that knowledge was up to him. But one thing she knew, it was time he met Maddie Grace.

Silence stretched between them.

"Vik?"

"I am…honored."

"Good." That was better than thinking she was a fool for believing in the emotion.

"You…I…" For the first time in memory, Vik didn't sound in complete control of his words or his thoughts.

"I don't expect you to say it back."

"Good." The relief in his tone was not complimentary, but she wasn't surprised by it, either.

"You'll never lie to me," she said, as if just making that revelation.

But maybe she understood the depth of his commitment to honesty between them fully for the first time.

"No, I will not."

That included not claiming to love her when he didn't, but it also meant that his promises? Were written in concrete as far as Viktor Beck was concerned.

CHAPTER NINE

MADDIE WAS SHOCKED when her father called and asked her to come to dinner. Alone.

They ate in the formal dining room. Even with the leaves removed from the table, it would easily seat six.

Maddie sat to her father's left and swirled her soup with her spoon, pretending to eat.

Her father didn't seem any more at ease than she felt.

Finally she gave in and asked, "Why am I here?"

"It's been a long time since we had a family dinner."

"There's a two-page magazine spread to prove otherwise."

He shook his head, an expression she couldn't quite decipher on his familiar features. "That is not the same."

"I'm not sure what you mean then."

"You and me. Family."

"We stopped being a family when Mom died." She didn't say it with accusation, or even anger.

He could thank the therapist he didn't know about for that, but it was still the truth.

"It was never my intention for that to happen."

She couldn't hold back a small scoffing sound. "You sent me to boarding school within months of her death. I'd say your intentions were pretty clear."

"That was a mistake."

Something inside Maddie cracked at that admission, but she merely shrugged. What could she say? *Yes, it had been a huge, painful mistake.*

Somehow agreeing didn't seem like the thing to do, though. Not least of which because no acknowledgment now could change the consequences of his choice when she was fifteen.

"I didn't know what to do," he admitted with a candidness rare for Jeremy Archer. "I failed your mother and I was terrified of failing you, so I sent you away, hoping they could do for you at school what I was so clearly not qualified to do at home."

Maddie stared at him as an emotional maelstrom swirled inside her. "Who are you and what have you done with my father?"

It was an old joke, but *man,* was it appropriate.

Her dad barked out a laugh. "I told Viktor this wouldn't be easy."

"He wanted you to talk to me?" Why wasn't she surprised?

"Yes." Jeremy sighed. "Viktor thinks our relationship is salvageable."

"He's an optimist."

"He is."

Giving up on the pretense of eating, she set her spoon down. "You sound surprised by that fact."

"It's not a side of him I noticed before."

"You don't think his business world-domination plans take optimism?" she asked, only partially tongue in cheek.

Her dad laughed again, this time longer and with more real humor. "I suppose they do."

"I guess that makes you something of an optimist, too." Which wasn't something she'd ever acknowledged before.

"Enough of one to believe things could be different for you than Helene." He sounded like he meant it.

"We all have our demons. I'm learning to cope with mine without jumping out of airplanes." Maddie could give him that at least.

Her father took a ruminative sip of his wine. "I used to think Helene got into trouble just to get my attention. She seemed to take a perverse pleasure in being written up in the media."

"She did."

He looked startled at Maddie's agreement. "But she was a risk taker before we ever met. You know that, don't you?"

"She used to tell me stories over her scrapbooks." It had all sounded so thrilling to a young girl.

Jeremy nodded. "It was one of the things I admired about her."

"You weren't the first important man in her life to ignore her." That was one of the things Maddie had come to realize.

Helene Madison had craved her own father's attention and only managed to get it when she acted out. By the time she married Jeremy Archer, the attention-seeking behavior was an already established coping mechanism.

"You're saying Helene wasn't adventurous by nature, but because her exploits got her father's attention."

"Oh, I think Mom was definitely adventurous, she just discovered that in giving in to that side of her personality, she got something she craved."

"She always said she understood the amount of time I had to give to my company."

"Would you have listened if she said she didn't?" He certainly hadn't responded to Maddie's verbal pleas for his time, or to return home from boarding school.

"Probably not," her father admitted with more honesty than she expected.

"Her death wasn't your fault." It was a truth that had been very hard come by for Maddie.

She'd blamed her dad for so long, but one of the first breakthroughs she'd made with her therapist was the realization that Helene Archer had been responsible for her own choices.

"Wasn't it?"

"No."

He didn't look like he agreed.

"Do you think Mom went racing because she didn't love me enough to want to be around to raise me?" Maddie asked.

Her dad went pale with shock, his eyes dilating, his mouth going slack for a second before he nearly shouted, "No, of course not. She adored you, Madison. You must know that."

"But she still went racing on the water at night."

"Not because of you."

"And not because of you, either."

"But—"

"Mom was an adult woman who suppressed normal caution for the adrenaline spikes that made her feel alive." The fact it had the side effect of gaining her the attention she craved only made her mom's adventures doubly irresistible to her.

"You sound like a psychologist."

"A degree in early childhood development has its share of psych courses." Maddie wasn't telling Jeremy about her sessions with a therapist.

She wasn't ashamed of seeing Dr. MacKenzie, but Maddie didn't trust her father enough to share the more private parts of her life with him. Not even this *new and improved* Jeremy.

She didn't know how deep the changes went or how long they would last.

Her dad's eyes—the same shade as her own, but without the vulnerability she saw in the mirror when she was alone—flickered with something between speculation and curiosity.

"Speaking of your mother," he said in a more familiar tone that revealed no emotion.

"Yes?"

"You and Viktor have chosen her birthday for your wedding date."

"Yes." A month before Maddie turned twenty-five, it had just felt right to speak their vows on a date connected in such a special way to her mom.

"Viktor said you wanted to honor her memory with the date."

"We do." Did her dad find that uncomfortable? Neither she nor Vik had considered that possibility.

Her father smiled, the expression appearing genuine. "I was hoping you would be willing to honor her memory in another way as well."

"How?" she asked warily.

"Do not worry, I am not going to use your mother's memory to try to guilt you into withdrawing the paperwork giving company shares to Ramona Grayson upon your twenty-fifth birthday."

But he hadn't forgotten it, either.

"It wouldn't work anyway. Mom loved Romi and I personally wouldn't have survived boarding school if her father hadn't sent her there, too."

Maddie had desperately wanted her SBC to come to the school once she'd realized her father wouldn't budge about her going there. However she'd never asked. It wouldn't have been fair. Just like Maddie, Romi had a life in San Francisco.

But Romi had begged her dad to send her and he'd done so.

Jeremy nodded. "He sent her because I offered to pay the tuition and dorm fees."

"No." Wouldn't her father have told her that before this?

"Yes. He told me when Romi came to him and asked to follow you. He didn't want to send her, but I thought you would both be better off with each other than your fathers."

Maddie's dad was sounding more and more human by the minute. She wasn't sure how she felt about that, but she thought it might be hope.

However, she felt compelled to say, "Mr. Grayson always loved Romi."

"But he was already drinking heavily by then. Do you think he was any more aware of his daughter's needs than I was of yours?"

No, the man who had fallen asleep drunk most nights had not been aware of what Romi needed.

"If she hadn't gone to boarding school, she

would have become her dad's caregiver." Jeremy sounded very certain of that. "Romi needed to get away and Gray needed to pour *himself* into bed at night."

"You used to be his friend."

"I still am, as much as you can befriend a man intent on drinking himself into an early grave and his own business into bankruptcy."

Worry creased Maddie's brow. "It's not that bad."

"Yet. But it will be."

"Don't pretend threatening to take his company over was a favor you would do him."

"No, it wouldn't be a favor to Grayson, but it would be to Romi." Her dad sounded very sure of that assertion.

"So you say."

"You don't trust me at all, do you?"

"Not really, no." She couldn't even say that if she thought the welfare of AIH was a given that her dad would put hers next.

She wasn't convinced of that.

Rather than appear upset by her denial, her dad shrugged. "Maybe you are right not to."

"That's not a comforting thing for you to say."

He shrugged. "Would you rather I lied?"

"No, but you would, if you thought it would get you what you wanted."

"That's one of the primary differences between

Viktor and I. Our business peers know it, too. If I want another company president to believe something, I make sure he hears it from Viktor."

"Has he ever lied for you unknowingly?" she asked, not sure she wanted to know the answer.

"No. I'm not saying I haven't been tempted, but while I may not feel the same compunction for truth that my successor does, I do recognize that if I did that and Viktor found out about it, he would find another vehicle for his ambition than AIH."

Well, she'd never considered her father to be stupid. "I think you're right."

"I know I am."

"So, about Mom's memory…" Maddie said, ready to get back to the reason for her presence at her father's dinner table.

"She always said she wanted you to wear her wedding dress when you married."

"You still have it?" Maddie couldn't hide the eagerness in her tone.

If she'd been with Vik, she wouldn't have even felt the need to try.

"Of course."

"But you got rid of all her things." Maddie would never forget coming home for the first time from boarding school to find most of the house redecorated and her mother's things gone.

"I kept her wedding dress and her jewelry for

you." Her father's tone implied he didn't understand why Maddie wouldn't know that.

"Why? When you got rid of everything else?"

"The dress is a piece of history."

"Not business history." So, why would her dad
care?

"Family history. A famous designer created
it for your great-grandmother in 1957, the year
after he did a similar dress for an actress in one
of her more famous roles." Jeremy cleared his
throat almost as if talking about this was making him emotional. "Every generation in her direct line has worn it since."

"I know."

"Oh, I thought maybe you'd forgotten. You
didn't mention wearing it."

"I thought you'd gotten rid of it."

"I didn't."

"I'm so glad." It was a dream she'd thought
would have to die with her mother.

"You're very much of a size with your mother.
I doubt it will require much tailoring."

The beautiful ivory strapless gown with embroi-
dery in champagne silk thread around the full
skirt and on the bodice required no altering at
all.

Though she and Romi agreed Maddie should
wear a corset under the embroidered bodice for

smooth lines. The champagne lining flipped over the hem as a contrast lay exactly as it was supposed to.

"You look so beautiful," Romi said with suspiciously shiny eyes.

The dress hugged Maddie's breasts and torso, nipping in at her natural waist and then flaring in a full skirt shorter in the front than the back, which had an understated train that swept the floor elegantly behind her.

"I look like my mom."

"But you have your dad's eyes." Romi twisted her mouth comically. "I can't believe he paid for me to attend boarding school with you."

"Me, either." But Mr. Grayson had confirmed Jeremy's claim.

"He loves you, I always said so."

"In his own way," Maddie agreed. "Just not the way I needed."

"Maybe he just didn't know how. From what you've told me about his parents, it doesn't sound like the Archers were a warm family."

Maddie had only a few memories of grandparents who were both dead by the time she turned five, but none of them included a hug, or a kiss, or any other sign of affection.

"You could be right, but Jeremy admitted he'd lie if it got him what he wanted."

"Well, you knew that."

"I did. It was just weird having him admit it. I guess he has his own personal brand of honesty, too."

Romi adjusted the folds of Maddie's skirt just so. "I suppose. I prefer Viktor's."

"Me, too," Maddie said fervently.

Both women laughed, and it felt good.

But then most things felt pretty amazing right now. Maddie was marrying the man she loved and even if he didn't love her, he'd promised a *real* family.

And Vik kept his promises.

Viktor walked down the elementary school's hallway behind an office aide who had agreed to escort him to Miss Jewett's first-grade classroom.

Unlike Madison, Viktor and Maxwell had attended public school, but in an area more affluent than this one. The mix of children and teachers here reflected San Francisco's varied population like the rarified social strata of the Archers did not.

Viktor wasn't sure why Madison had asked him to meet her here. She'd said something about wanting to talk to him with the help of a visual aid.

He didn't know what that meant. He couldn't see how an overcrowded public school would work as inspiration for her charter school. Unless it was the success they had with their volunteer program.

He'd done a little research before leaving the office on this grade school and discovered that they had a significantly higher than usual rate of parent participation in the classroom as well as other volunteerism.

When he'd arrived at the office, it was to discover that he was expected. So, he was definitely in the right place.

Whatever Madison's reasons for having him there.

He noticed two things immediately after the aide opened the classroom's door—Madison looking very unlike herself and the absolute silence he did not associate with a roomful of children.

Wearing a mousy brown wig, contacts that obscured the Mediterranean blue of her eyes with brown and clothes clearly bought off the rack at a box store, his fiancée sat at a small desk in a circle with six students.

Tattered books with brightly colored pictures, large print and few words were open on the desks in front of the children. Madison held her own copy, a smile frozen on her face as she met his gaze.

Vik allowed one brow to rise in query. "Hello, Madison. It appears you have some friends I haven't met."

Her fixed smile morphed into a genuine grin as she jumped to her feet. "You're early."

He couldn't help noticing the cheap cotton top and denim jeans she wore showed off her curves in ways that affected his libido as surely as her designer dresses.

He didn't like the wig or colored contacts, though.

He shrugged away her comment about his timing. "Introduce me."

"Of course."

Not wanting to intimidate the children with his size, Viktor dropped to one knee and reached to shake hands with each child as Maddie introduced them.

A few returned his greeting with charming politeness. One small girl, clearly Madison's favorite from the way the small girl tucked herself behind his fiancée's legs, ducked her head, but wiggled her fingers in a shy hello.

Viktor met the teacher and the parent volunteer as well.

"Very nice to meet you," he said to Miss Jewett.

"The pleasure is all ours." She smiled, her eyes warm as they lit on Madison. "Your fiancée is a fantastic volunteer. She's so good with the children and could be a teacher with her credentials."

"I am aware." He just hadn't been aware that she volunteered in the public school system.

Did her father know?

Madison clearly didn't want to leave right

away, so Viktor stayed, enjoying the time helping six-year-olds with their reading.

They were in his Jaguar and headed toward the other side of the city when she finally pulled off the offensive wig, exposing her red curls crushed in a messy pile. It reminded him of the way she looked after sex, the only time she was completely disheveled—Madison woke looking more tempting than ever.

She rubbed at her scalp and ran her fingers through her hair, causing some curls to bounce up again. "It's always such a relief to get that thing off."

"Why do you wear it?"

"Because *Maddie Grace* is a normal woman with a degree and desire to volunteer with children. She doesn't get written up in the tabloids or followed by the paparazzi."

"And that's important to you?"

"To be normal? It was when I started. Now, it's just easier. Can you imagine what the media would make of the billionaire heiress as a volunteer teacher's aide?"

"I have a feeling we're going to find out."

"That's what I thought. With our marriage and the vestiges of Perrygate, I kind of figured it was only a matter of time before my secret got exposed."

"Some secret." She was even more wonderful

than he'd always known. "How long have you been volunteering like this?"

"It started as a dare with Romi. Trying to attend a political rally incognito. It worked and I got the idea to volunteer at a soup kitchen the next weekend *dressed up*."

"Don't you mean dressed down?"

She laughed, the sound soft and more enticing than he was sure she meant it to be. "I guess."

"It might be a good idea to come clean before some enterprising reporter does it for you."

"I guess," she said again, not sounding nearly as amused or enthusiastic.

"As much as you enjoy being Maddie Grace, Madison Beck will be able to effect more widespread change and influence." Just giving Madison his last name verbally was satisfying in a way Viktor didn't understand or analyze.

"But will she get to teach a first-grader how to read?"

"Yes. That's what the charter school is about, right? Helping children one-on-one."

"It is." He could hear the smile in Madison's voice.

"So Grace for Romi Grayson?"

"No, my grandmother Madison."

"That's right." He'd forgotten.

"You don't mind?"

He pulled into a parking spot on the side of

the road, wanting to have this conversation face-to-face. Cutting the engine, he turned to face her.

Brown eyes stared back at him and he frowned. "Can you take those out?"

"What? Oh…" Comprehension dawned.

She pulled a small case from her backpack, so different than the trendy designer bags he usually saw her wear, and proceeded to take out and store away the contacts.

"This persona, she's more you than the famous designer wedding dress?"

"Sometimes. Sometimes I just really love my Chanel, you know?" Madison's pretty bow lips twisted in a wry grimace. "I like to pretend that I couldn't care less about the latest fashions and keep up with them just to be Madison *Archer*, but the truth is? I like both."

He nodded. Not because he understood. He wore tailored designer suits as a sign of power, not because he thought about how they looked. But because he was glad Madison Archer, soon to be Madison Beck, wasn't someone she didn't want to be.

"So, the question was *do I mind?* Yes?"

Madison's beautiful blue eyes shone at him. "Yes."

"Do I mind that I am going to marry a woman who cares so much about helping others she has created an alternate persona so she can do it? No, Madison. I do not mind at all."

Giving in to the urge that seemed to grow with each passing day, Viktor leaned across the console and kissed Madison.

He lifted his mouth to say, "In fact, I think it's amazing."

Madison sighed and leaned back into the kiss, delight radiating off of her and twisting its way around Viktor's heart.

Viktor's *deda* and *babulya* had them over for dinner a couple of days later and dropped their own bombshell.

Stunned at his grandparents' request, Viktor could only ask, "You want us to what?"

"When we moved here, we gave up all the old ways," Misha said. "We changed our last name from Bezukladnikov to Beck—we even changed our baby boy's name from Ivan to Frank. Very American."

"I know all this." It was family history he had shared with Madison years ago.

Her lovely face expressed memory of the event too. Viktor just didn't understand why his *deda* felt the need to rehash those realities now.

"We did not speak Russian in our home. We encouraged our little Ivan to become fully American." *Babulya's* voice broke on his father's original name. "Frank, who spoke without an accent and did all the things the other children at school did."

"You wanted him to embrace and be embraced by his new homeland," Madison offered in understanding while Viktor reeled with alien confusion.

His grandmother smiled appreciatively. "Exactly, but we gave away too much and he became the man he is today."

"A flake. You can say it, *Babulya*." Vik frowned with frustration, really not liking the idea his beloved grandparents were trying to take responsibility for his father's lifetime of selfish and poor choices. "My dad is a deadbeat."

"Do not speak of your father that way," Misha said, but with little heat.

Viktor didn't argue, but he didn't promise not to, either. He couldn't.

Madison looked at him with something far more attractive than compassion. Her eyes glowed that way they did when she called him her white knight. Viktor had no clue what in this particular situation would put that look on her face, but he would not question the obvious lack of the one emotion he hated above all others.

Pity.

His *babulya's* eyes usually filled with a tranquility he'd always relied on, but now shimmered with regret. "We think we let go of too many traditions and he felt himself cast adrift."

"Oh, for…" Viktor clenched his jaw to bite back the first words that came to his mind. "Dad did not become a con artist because he didn't have a traditional Russian wedding. The one right and good thing he did in his life was his marriage to my mom."

"That is not true," Misha said in a deep voice so like Viktor's own. "He fathered you."

Viktor opened his mouth and shut it again without a word.

Madison grinned, a smug glint in her azure eyes. "I told him the same thing."

"You are a very good match for our grandson." His grandmother's answering smile was blinding. "It pleases Misha and me very much that you appreciate our Viktor as we do."

"He's easy to love."

Once again Viktor did not know how to respond to those words, though he liked hearing them. Very much.

But love was not something he had ever considered in the equation of his marriage to Madison and the life they would build together. Was it enough that she felt the emotion, or did she expect him to reciprocate one day?

Could he? Did he even know how?

He had never been in love before. The affection between his grandparents had grown over time and did not look on the surface anything like the passion that burned between Viktor and Madison.

The silence had stretched and it should have been awkward, but the three most important people in the world to him simply observed Viktor with varying degrees of understanding.

It was a strange experience, but not unpleasant.

"Thank you," he finally said to Madison, hoping that once again it was enough.

His grandfather winced, but patted Viktor on the shoulder. Misha didn't say anything, though.

Madison's smile turned soft in a way Viktor did not understand, but liked nonetheless.

His grandmother rolled her eyes. "Viktor, my dear grandson, you have much to learn about romance."

Viktor could not deny it.

She didn't seem to expect an answer. "Is it so much to ask you follow a few of our family's traditions?"

"I'm not answering before you tell me exactly which ones you're talking about." His caution was necessary.

Russian wedding preparations and celebrations could become extremely complicated and involved.

But his grandparents' requests weren't unreasonable, even if they did mean Madison had to spend the night before her wedding at Jeremy's home instead of Viktor's bed.

Five weeks after Perry's exposé, Maddie waited in the drawing room of her father's mansion the morning of her wedding.

She was wearing the gown her mother had worn, and her mother before that and *her* mother before that in 1957.

Her full-length Victorian-era veil of Brussels lace was even older than the dress. Romi had shown up with it a week ago. And it was the exact same ivory as the gown.

Romi adjusted the veil around Maddie's face now. "You are so beautiful."

Maddie couldn't answer. If she tried to talk, her emotions were going to get the best of her.

"Viktor is going to be here any minute. Are you ready?"

Maddie indicated herself with a wave of her hand and forced an even tone. "What do you think?"

"I already told you, beautiful. But, sweetie, that's not what I'm talking about. Are *you* ready?"

"According to Vik, we got married that day we made promises overlooking San Francisco's skyline."

"Pffft." Romi shook her head. "Men."

"Those promises were vows." Of that Maddie was very certain.

"So are the words you're going to speak today."

Maddie nodded. "I'm ready."

"You love him."

"I do." There was no point in denying it. Besides Romi could always tell when Maddie was lying.

"You always have."

Maddie wasn't so sure about that, but she couldn't deny she'd never fallen in love with anyone else.

"Perry didn't stand a chance."

"He didn't want one." Their friendship had never been like that.

"I'm not so sure about that."

"It doesn't matter."

"No," Romi said with finality. "It doesn't."

Maddie grinned at her sister-by-choice. "I'm getting married today."

"You are." Romi grinned back.

Their hug was fierce enough to crush silk and neither of them cared.

The sound of the doorbell came faintly from the hall. Then Vik's voice and Misha's laugh.

Oh, this was real. It was happening. Now.

More laughter and then the door to the drawing room swung in and bounced against the wall.

Her six-foot-two distant cousin James, wearing a distinctly masculine tuxedo and tulle veil, stumbled in first. "He figured out I wasn't you, cuz."

Maddie found herself laughing along with the others as they came in behind him. The first tradition had been observed. Her father had pretended to offer an alternate "bride" and Vik had shown his determination to only wed one.

Misha, looking dapper in his own tux, and Ana, beautiful in her rose-pink suit, came in behind James. Maddie's father wore a traditional morning coat and ascot, but Vik was in breath-stealing Armani.

James's parents were there, too, along with the second cousins who had been at the family engagement dinner. Vik's aunt, his father's younger sister by ten years, and her two teenagers had flown in from New York. Frank hadn't made it.

The cousins from Russia had extended their stay in California, though, so they were here as well.

Enough family to please Misha and Ana's need for traditions to be observed, Maddie hoped.

But really? As far as she was concerned, no one else mattered, not when Vik came to stand in front of her, his expression hungry, approving and supremely satisfied all at once.

"Ti takAya krasIvaya." Vik reached out to

touch her, but his hand hovered in the air between them, not quite connecting.

"He is telling you that you are beautiful," Misha informed her.

Maddie nodded her understanding, but couldn't look away from the intensity in Vik's espresso gaze.

"I have come to ransom my bride," he said in formal tones clearly meant for her father, but Vik's attention never strayed from Maddie.

"Your father tried pawning this one off on us," Misha said, pointing at James. "But my grandson is too observant to be fooled."

Because anyone would have mistaken her tall, *male* cousin for her.

But Maddie laughed because it was supposed to be in fun and she found she enjoyed this Russian tradition very much.

Vik offered an open Tiffany box with a sapphire-studded tiepin and cuff links resting on the cream satin.

Her father accepted it with what sounded like genuine thanks, but then he shook his head. "This is not enough."

And she knew that was part of the ritual Misha and Ana wanted to see observed.

Misha made a production of arguing the merits of the gentlemen's jewelry, but Vik never even cracked a smile. His powerful focus was entirely on Maddie and she felt a connection to him that was more spiritual than humorous.

Finally, Misha came between them, offering her another Tiffany box. This one contained a five-strand pearl necklace and perfectly matched pearl studs in a vintage inspired gold setting.

Her gaze flicked between the pearls and Vik and then to Romi, because Maddie's SBC had convinced her to go without a necklace. "You knew."

Romi nodded, her brilliant smile watery.

Maddie reached up and removed her mother's diamond earrings and handed them to Romi, who she now realized had left her own ears bare just for this. It was right that Romi would be wearing something of Helene's at Maddie's wedding.

Vik helped Maddie put on the earrings and the necklace, the moment unbearably intimate. When he was done, he bent down and placed a barely there kiss against her lips before carefully dropping her veil back into place.

"Now, there can be a wedding," Misha said with hearty satisfaction.

CHAPTER TEN

THEY TOOK TWO limos to the church.

Maddie didn't pay attention to who went where except that she had Vik on one side of her and Romi on the other.

The Holy Virgin Cathedral looked like it had been transplanted right out of Russia, with its cross-topped triple-domed spires and white facade. The inside was awe-inspiring, with its domed ceilings decorated with iconography and the ornate public altar area.

She lost herself in the beauty of the service, but nothing was as moving as the moment before the crowning ceremony when Vik sidestepped tradition and lifted her veil to kiss her again and whisper that now even God knew she was his.

The words might be considered irreverent by some, but they settled in Maddie's soul. He left her veil folded back so that when the crown was placed on her head signifying the sacrament, Maddie felt both bound and freed at the same time.

They skipped the civil ceremony that would have been required to make the wedding legal in Russia because it wasn't necessary in America. Consequently, they broke crystal glasses at the reception in front of a few hundred of her father and Vik's nearest and dearest.

Both glasses shattered into rubble, though there could be no doubt that Vik threw his with an impressive force beyond what Maddie used. Everyone cheered.

"It will be a long and blessed union," Misha announced loudly.

She was a little surprised to discover the man hired to be toastmaster was a well-known Shakespearean actor, and one of her favorite up-and-coming performers sang for the guest's enjoyment.

They ate, cut the cake and toast after toast was made to the happy couple.

It was all sort of overwhelming and amazing. Nothing about this wedding felt like a business arrangement. When she mentioned that to Vik, he smiled.

"Because this marriage is *not* a business arrangement," he said firmly.

"But—"

"It's a marriage of dreams. Accept that for what it is."

Happier than she had ever been, Maddie

nodded and did just that. She wasn't at all surprised when Romi caught her bouquet.

Maddie had been aiming after all.

What was surprising and even a little worrisome, was that Maxwell Black caught the garter. The look he gave Romi would have had Maddie running for the hills, but her friend just blushed. And looked more than a little interested.

Huh. That was something to think about.

After Maddie's own honeymoon.

She smiled so much during the reception that her cheeks hurt by the time the white Rolls-Royce arrived to take them away.

Maddie was surprised when the car pulled up in front of the Ritz-Carlton instead of Parean Hall.

She turned to Vik. "I thought we were going home."

"I like the sound of that."

"Going home?" she asked, confused and not minding a bit.

"Home. *Our home*," he emphasized.

Heat she did not understand crept into Maddie's cheeks. "But we aren't there."

"No, we are here. And this moment the only three people who know that are you, me and the driver." Vik sounded very proud of that fact.

"What about security?"

"Not even them. Not tonight. No friends. No family. No security. *No press.*"

Delight suffused her. "Tonight is ours."

"Yes."

"I like it."

"Good."

He carried her over the threshold of Suite 919, one of the two most luxurious sets of rooms on the club level.

Its beauty was lost on Maddie, though. She was way too focused on Vik to pay attention to marble floors and Chippendale furniture.

"Champagne?" he asked without putting her down.

She shook her head.

"Snack?"

A smile flirted at her mouth as she said primly, "No thank you."

His eyes darkened with primal intent. "Bed then?"

"Oh, yes."

He carried her into the bedroom and lowered her to her feet. "Did I tell you how lovely you are today?"

"You may have mentioned it, yes."

He nodded, as if in serious contemplation. "I can only imagine one circumstance in which you could be more breathtaking."

"Yes?" she asked.

"Let me show you."

"Okay," she breathed out.

He removed her crown and veil with careful, deliberate movements. Then he took off the jewelry he'd helped her put on earlier.

"I don't think I told you. The pearls are exquisite. Thank you."

"They are just little white beads until you are wearing them."

"Oh, wow...I don't know even know how to take some of the things you say."

"As truth. We've established I do not lie to you." He brushed his lips over the back of her neck.

She did nothing to suppress the shiver the small touch elicited. "Or at all, according to Jeremy."

Vik came around and faced her, and then leaned down to press their mouths together softly for only a brief moment. "Or at all." He kissed down her neck and along her bare shoulder.

Each caress of his lips left a trail of goose bumps in its wake and she was trembling with desire by the time he made it around to the back of her dress.

He undid the bodice, trailing kisses down her spine as he did so.

The silk of her corset was no barrier between his lips and her skin. He helped her step out of the dress and then took the time to carry it into the dining room and lay it on the table.

When he came back into the bedroom, she said, "Thank you."

He looked at her questioningly.

"For caring about my dress."

He shrugged as if his consideration wasn't important, or maybe rather that it should be taken for granted. "It is a living memory for your family."

She hoped she never stopped appreciating the big, but especially little things he did to take care of her.

"So, is this what you were talking about?" she asked with a sweeping gesture toward herself with her hand.

Maddie stood before Vik in her corset, panties, sheer silk thigh highs and glittery Jimmy Choo heels, but nothing else.

His smile was predatory when he shook his head. "Almost, but not quite."

She stepped out of her heels.

"Closer." Sensuality oozed through his voice.

She swallowed. They'd made love every night for the past five weeks, so nothing about this one should make her nervous.

But as much as he'd claimed to consider their promises at the Marin Headlands overlook to be enough to bind them, the look of possession in his eyes was about ten times more intense than it had been the past weeks.

She reached down to unhook her stockings, but he put a staying hand. "Let me."

"Okay." She straightened and waited.

With no consideration for the expensive fabric of his tuxedo trousers, Vik knelt in front of her. But rather than undoing the slide button holding her stocking in place, he settled his big hands on her hips and leaned forward to press a kiss between her breasts.

Her breath caught and her knees went weak. "Vik, please."

"Please what?" he asked, his voice dark with passion. "This?"

He nuzzled the slopes of her breasts, his tongue flicking out to taste her skin. Little sparks of pleasure chased the path he took with his mouth.

His hands slid around to cup her bottom and then fingertips teased the exposed skin between the bottom of her panties and the tops of her stockings.

She only realized he'd undone the hooks when the soft silk slid down first one thigh and then another—with a little help from Vik.

Over a month ago, she'd never been touched like this, but now her body knew the delight to be had. She felt empty inside in a way she never had before she'd known what it was like to be filled up.

Her thighs quivered with brush of his fingertips while part of her craved even more. Firmer
touch, more intimate caresses.

Her nipples had already drawn tight in antici-
pation of his attention.

Images of what he'd done before melded with
the present to intensify every brush of skin
against skin.

Vik reached behind her to undo the corset and
she was grateful she'd gone for one with a zipper rather than laces. It parted and came away
from her overheated skin in a matter of seconds.

"Mmmm…" he hummed, his expression both
pleased and predatory. "Almost there."

There was no surprise when he hooked his fingers in the waistband of her panties and tugged
them down. Only a sense of breathless antici-
pation.

With one final kiss on each of her nipples, he
stood. "Now, that is the most beautiful sight I
could ever imagine."

Heat suffused her body; she'd lost her ability
to suppress her blushes around this man.

None of her defense mechanisms came naturally around Vik anymore.

"You're still dressed." Her voice sounded like
a croaking frog.

"Would you like to change that?" he asked,
his tone filled with sensual challenge.

In answer, she stepped forward and undid his bow tie.

"I'm starting to understand how you feel about unwrapping gifts," she said as she pulled the tie slowly from the starched collar of his shirt.

"Yes?"

"Oh, yes." She took her time on the buttons as well, leaning forward to inhale his masculine scent and nuzzle the chest hair not covered by his white silk undershirt.

Maddie reveled in each new inch of golden skin revealed, taking her time to touch and kiss as he had done.

Funny how quickly she'd gained the confidence to do this, but then he'd never reacted with anything but all-out enthusiasm to any sexual overture she made. No matter how small.

When she had him completely naked, she stepped forward so their bodies were flush. He was so much bigger than her and yet they fit together like they'd been created as adjoining pieces of a puzzle.

They kissed for several very satisfying minutes, no sense of urgency, just pleasure as they connected as intimately as when he was inside her.

But there was something she wanted to do, something she hadn't yet tried, something that intrigued, but also intimidated her.

What better time to take the plunge but on her wedding night?

She pulled back to break the kiss, but he drew her back in. This happened a few more times before she finally managed to separate their lips and bodies.

"I want to taste you," she told him.

A supernova flared in his eyes. "I'm not about to tell you no."

"I didn't think you would." She dropped to her knees in front of him.

"Wouldn't you be more comfortable on the bed?" he asked, sounding like it really mattered to him.

And she knew it did.

She took his large erection in her hand and caressed up and down. "Maybe, but not yet." Maddie stroked him a second time.

Groaning, Vik swayed.

She loved the velvety smoothness of his skin here and knowing that small touch affected him in such a primal way.

Leaning forward, Maddie took her first real taste of Vik's straining sex. The skin should taste like any other skin on his body, but it was even more addictive to her taste buds.

Drops of preejaculate burst with flavor on her tongue and she thought how she would be the only one who got to experience this. Never again would another woman know him in this way.

Only Maddie.

Vik was hers.

She swirled her tongue around the spongy skin of his head and he made a sound between a growl and a groan. "Please, *milaya moya*."

He could deny it, but the wedding made a difference to Vik. He'd never spoken in Russian to, or around her, before today. He was bringing her into his inner sanctum.

And that was as alluring as the naked man in front of her.

"What does that mean?" she asked, tipping her head back to see his face.

Their gazes locked, his dark eyes filled with passion.

"My sweet." His hips canted forward, seemingly of their own accord, and the tip of his erection brushed her lips.

She took him into her mouth, bringing forth another deep sound of pleasure from Vik. Hollowing her cheeks, Maddie sucked, moving her mouth forward and backward, but never so far forward she choked.

His hands settled softly against her head, but he made no effort to hold her in place or guide her movements. It was like he was giving her silent approval, as if he thought maybe his sounds of pleasure weren't enough.

It was wonderful, but her jaw got sore faster than she expected and she had to pull back.

"That was amazing," he said with apparent sincerity.

She smiled up at him. "Short, you mean."

He laughed, the sound husky. "Much longer and I would have come."

"You're easy."

"For you? Definitely." Vik pulled her to her feet and right into a mind-numbing kiss.

Not just easy, but *hungry*.

She hadn't known that missing a single night of lovemaking would make him so impatient, so ravenous for her and the pleasure they created together.

But Vik lost no time backing her up to the bed. He ripped the coverlet and top sheet off with a single, powerful yank and then maneuvered them onto the center of the king-sized mattress.

He guided her legs apart, her knees bent and she expected immediate penetration. What she got was his mouth against her most intimate flesh.

In moments, she was writhing with the need to climax, but an even stronger desire to have him inside her.

"Please, Vik. Make love to me now."

His head came up, eyes nearly black with passion meeting hers. "What do you think I am doing?"

"Not like that."

"Oh, yes, like this."

"But I'm going to come." Desperation overrode her every inhibition.

"Yes, you will," he promised in a sexy growl.

"But—"

"At least once."

Then he went back to what he was doing, taking her to the edge and over, her cries echoing around them in the luxurious bedroom. His tongue laved her gently through aftershocks until her body went boneless, her legs flopping down to the bed.

He pulled the sheet from its tangle with the comforter and wiped his mouth on it before surging up and over her. "Condom, or no condom?" he asked.

They'd been lucky and their first time without protection hadn't resulted in pregnancy. He'd been very careful to use condoms since.

But they were married now and had agreed to start a family right away. Equally important to her, she wanted the intimacy of no barrier between them.

"No birth control."

He nodded, if anything, his expression turning even more feral with a voracious sexual need. His desire came off him in waves and he still managed to enter her carefully, giving her most sensitive flesh a chance to adjust to his granite-hard erection filling her.

After her recent explosive climax and the way he incited aftershocks until she simply couldn't respond anymore, she'd been prepared to share the intimacy with him and revel in the emotional connection. But not much more.

Maddie was not prepared for the way her body reacted to their joining. The physical ecstasy ignited again, as if it had never been banked, burning hotter with every movement of his body in hers. Pleasure that she should be too sated to feel rolled through her, making her womb spasm and the muscles around his hardness contract.

He set a slow, but thoroughly penetrating rhythm that built the ecstasy inside her until she was on the verge of another inconceivable orgasm.

As if he could read her mind, or maybe it was just the clues her body was giving him, Vik sped up, pounding into her, jolts of pleasure going through her on every thrust.

He stared down at her, his face a rictus of sexual ecstasy, his coffee-brown eyes burning with demand. "Come now, *milaya moya*."

And improbably…she did, screaming as rapture sent her body into tremors that could have toppled cities.

He went completely rigid and joined her in

the ultimate sexual pleasure, their gazes as connected and intimate as the most passionate kiss.

"If that didn't make a baby…" she said breathlessly.

He pulled her close into his body. "We will keep trying with great delight."

Which they did for the rest of the night, falling into exhausted slumber after the sun lit the morning fog.

He woke her to shower at noon. Not alone. Showering together was one of her recently discovered perks to sharing physical intimacy with Vik.

They came out of the bathroom to find clothing lying across the freshly made bed.

A familiar black-and-white polka-dot set of hard-sided luggage was sitting against the wall beside a black fold over garment bag and matching leather duffel as well.

"How long are we staying here?" she asked as she donned her bra and then tugged on a black silk shell over it.

Vik flicked the suitcases a glance and then met her eyes. "We are checking out in an hour."

"Where are we going?" Not home.

Both their personal possessions had been moved to Parean Hall the day before the wedding. So, there would be no need for luggage.

He pulled on his briefs and then a pair of dark indigo designer jeans. "Palm Springs."

"Why?"

"Our honeymoon."

She stilled in her own efforts to get dressed. "But I thought we weren't going on a honeymoon."

"I do not recall agreeing to that."

"We never talked about it," she pointed out.

He pulled on a black-and-white Armani X polo. "It is traditional."

"Our marriage isn't exactly." The jeans she stepped into were a pair of her favorites.

"I disagree."

She shook her head, knowing he wouldn't budge on his outlook. Vik saw nothing odd in marrying a woman he didn't love so he could build a legacy for the children he most certainly would.

"So, Palm Springs."

His grin was knowing. "I saw little point in an exotic location when we are likely to spend most of our time in the bedroom."

Blushing, she ignored his assertion and shrugged into the burgundy-and-black colorblocked jacket someone had left out for her to wear. "I like Palm Springs."

In fact, the small resort city nestled in the California desert was one of Maddie's all-time favorite places. She used to visit with her mother every winter. There were enough celebrities that vacationed there, the Archers of the world were barely a blip on the media's radar.

Maddie had continued to travel to the desert when she needed to get away from being Madison Archer, notorious heiress.

Somehow, she thought Vik knew that.

He smiled. "It is a good thing you are as intelligent as you are, or the amount of school you missed traveling with your mother would have been a real problem."

"She always brought a tutor along and got my assignments."

Vik's expression turned heated. "I'll be the only tutor you'll need this week."

"After the last five weeks, and particularly last night, I'm pretty sure there isn't much for you to teach me."

"You'll be surprised."

Not "you could be" or "you might be," but "you will be" surprised. The man had no shortage of confidence.

And the following eight days proved how justified he was in that regard.

True to his word, they spent *a lot* of time in the bedroom of their suite at an oasis-style resort outside of the city. However, Vik also insisted on visiting Maddie's favorite spots, taking her to dine at some of the best restaurants in and around the city as well as shopping in the exclusive boutiques of top designers.

Maddie, who had always considered her socialite side something of a necessary evil, enjoyed herself in ways she hadn't in Palm Springs since Helene's death.

Vik was flatteringly enthusiastic about almost every article of clothing Maddie tried on, and even the growls that particularly revealing pieces elicited were flattering in their own way.

They returned to San Francisco to a list of possible properties for the charter school that Vik had his real estate agent compile.

Vik had too many things on his desk no one else could handle after a week's absence to accompany Maddie and Romi when they toured the properties. But he asked detailed questions each evening about what Maddie had seen, proving the sincerity of his interest in the project.

Friday morning, Maddie got a text from her father's assistant requesting she come to a meeting in his office that afternoon.

She was supposed to do another tour of the property she and Romi had pretty much decided was *the one* for the school. Feeling magnanimous toward the world in general, even her father, Maddie called and rescheduled the tour before texting the PA that she would be at the meeting.

Maddie was shown into her father's office by his secretary, who surprisingly did not stay to take notes. So, it was a personal meeting?

Only, why at his office?

Her dad stood and came around from behind his desk. "Madison. I would like you to meet Dr. Wilson, the director for…" Jeremy named a well-known institution that specialized in psychiatric studies.

It was then she noticed the other man in the room.

Gray-haired and distinguished-looking in a suit of good quality, if not an Italian designer label, Dr. Wilson was sitting in one of the armchairs that sat opposite a matching leather sofa on the other side of her father's office.

He rose now and walked to Maddie, putting his hand out for Maddie to shake. "Madison. It's a pleasure to meet you."

"Thank you. I hope I can say the same." Though she did not have a good feeling about this.

Why did her father have a psychiatrist in his office for their meeting?

"Let's all sit down and get comfortable," Dr. Wilson said, indicating he considered himself a key player in the meeting to come.

The fact that her father followed the doctor's lead without comment indicated he agreed.

Maddie wasn't feeling quite so acquiescent. She remained standing as her father took a position at one end of the sofa and the doctor returned to his leather armchair. "What is this about?"

"Sit down, Madison, so we can discuss this like civilized people."

"Tell me what we are discussing first," she demanded in a chilly tone she hadn't used in weeks.

Her father frowned. "You are being rude."

"And you are being cagey." When it came to her father?

Cagey was way worse than rude.

"Do you see what I mean?" Jeremy asked the doctor. "Unreasonably intractable."

"You've asked Dr. Wilson here to evaluate me?" Maddie demanded, emotion cracking through the facade of cool before she reined it in.

Surprisingly, her dad winced, but he nodded. "It has come to my attention that you've been seeing a therapist."

"I did for a few weeks, yes. Half of America has at one time or another." And her choice to do so was a good thing, not a weakness.

"That is actually a bit of an exaggeration," Dr. Wilson said, like he was making note of Maddie's tendency to overstate things. "The number is closer to twenty percent."

"Who told you I was seeing someone?" she asked Jeremy, ignoring the doctor.

Vik wouldn't have told him. He might not love Maddie, but he was her white knight. Vik would never sacrifice her to the king.

"Does Vik know about this meeting?" she demanded.

Her father gave her his game face. "What do you think?"

"That you don't want to answer my question." She pulled out her phone.

"Who are you calling?" Dr. Wilson asked, his tone overly patient.

"My husband."

"You see? Shades of codependency and paranoia," her father said.

Maddie wanted to throw her phone at his head, but didn't want to know what the psychiatrist would make of that. Vik's phone sent her to voice mail.

He must have been in a meeting.

She left a message. "It's me. Jeremy called me in for a meeting with a psychiatrist. I need to talk to you. Call me."

Dr. Wilson was watching her with an indecipherable expression. Her dad's eyes were narrowed, but she wasn't sure if it was with worry or annoyance.

"So, you know I saw a therapist and you've brought Dr. Wilson here to observe me. Why?"

"No one said I was here to observe you," the doctor said.

"No one said you weren't."

Neither the doctor nor her father answered that.

Finally, Jeremy said, "I've told Dr. Wilson my concerns about your increasingly erratic behavior over the years."

"And while I applaud your positive action in seeking help," Dr. Wilson said, as if speaking to a child, or an adult whose reasoning ability was compromised, "I must concur with your father that your actions since your mother's death indicate a spiraling condition."

"I do not have a condition." What she did have was a brain and it was starting to work. "You aren't going to prove me mentally incompetent to sign the paperwork giving Romi half of my shares in AIH. It's not going to work."

Her father's expression said he disagreed.

Even more ominously, the doctor shook his head. "Signing such a document as the one your father described to me in and of itself is hardly a rational action."

"You think not?"

"You think it is?"

"I know it is and I also know what I do with

my money and assets is not your business, Dr. Wilson, or for that matter, Jeremy Archer's."

"You call your father by his first name. That indicates a level of dissociation to those closest to you."

Who was this guy? Popping off with psychobabble on the basis of nothing but her father's obviously biased assertions and a few seconds conversation was not in any way professional.

"I'm closer to my cleaning lady than my father. In fact, I'm closer to *his* housekeeper than I am to him." And that might have been an exaggeration, but she defied either of them to prove differently.

The psychiatrist gave her a concerned look. "Your lack of emotional intimacy with your one remaining parent is certainly something we can explore together."

"Dr. Wilson, you are not and never will be *my* doctor. Now, if you two will excuse me." She turned to leave the office.

"Madison!" her father barked.

She didn't stop. He could leave whatever threat he wanted to make on her voice mail.

CHAPTER ELEVEN

MADDIE WAS IN the parking garage when her phone rang. Vik's ringtone.

She answered. "My father found out I was seeing a therapist."

"I didn't tell him."

"I didn't think you did."

"Good."

"I'm just…" Frustrated. Confused. Upset. "He wants to prove me incompetent to sign the papers giving Romi half my AIH shares."

"I had n—"

"There's something he didn't think of, I bet," she interrupted, not really hearing Vik.

"What is that?" Vik asked, sounding both cautious and concerned.

"If he gets a judge to say I wasn't competent to sign those papers. I wasn't competent to say my vows, either, and *we* aren't married. What will that do his precious plans to marry me off to his heir?" she demanded.

Vik made a sound like a growl. "That is not going to happen."

"I thought things were getting better with him."

"They are."

"If anyone has lost their mind it is him."

"I agree."

She nodded.

"Madison?"

"You're on my side, right?" Vik wouldn't support his mentor and friend in this, would he?

"Of course. You are my wife and you are staying that way."

Because he wanted control of AIH. Because he wanted the future he planned with her. Right that second, Maddie wished desperately there was another, more emotionally compelling reason for Vik to insist their marriage stood in validity.

Love.

She needed her husband's love. More than she wanted her father's acceptance. A lot more.

She couldn't really care less about Jeremy sliding back into old habits. However, suddenly the knowledge that the man she loved more than her own life appreciated her feelings but didn't share them hurt in a way she couldn't ignore.

"I need some time to think."

"What? Madison, where are you? I will come to you."

"No. I just…give me some time, Vik." She ended the call and then turned off her phone.

She didn't want to talk to anyone. Not even Romi.

Maddie got into her hybrid car—not exactly what an heiress might be expected to drive, but it was environmentally responsible—and drove to her favorite coffee shop/bookstore.

How was she going to live the rest of her life in love with her husband and knowing he didn't reciprocate her feelings. She didn't know if it was *couldn't* or *wouldn't*, but it didn't matter.

Maddie hadn't been to the coffee shop since before Perrygate, but she needed time to think and a place to do it in that Vik wouldn't think to look.

She got her usual order and took it to her favorite table positioned between a book stack and the window. Since the lower half of the window was painted with a mural that looked like old leather volumes on bookshelves, no one would see her from the outside.

Not unless they got right up to the window and looked down.

Her thoughts whirled in a mass of contradicting voices and images as her coffee cooled in its cup, but one idea rose to the surface again and again.

Vik *acted* like a man in love.

He couldn't get enough of her sexually. Maddie's happiness was very important to him. Given a choice, he *always* opted to spend time with her rather than away from her. He wanted her to be the mother of his children.

Did the words really matter?

She'd been doing fine without them to this point. But being thrown back into Ruthlessville by her father had undercut Maddie's sense of emotional security.

Did she really need Vik to admit he loved her for her to feel secure in her happiness with him?

She still had no answer to that question when she heard her name spoken in a masculine tone she'd never planned to hear again.

She looked up and frowned. "Go away, Perry."

"You don't take my calls or respond to my texts."

He was surprised? "I blocked your number."

"I figured that out."

"You aren't supposed to be talking to me."

"Nothing in the agreement that bastard you married got me to sign said I couldn't talk *to* you, only about you." Perry sounded really annoyed by that.

"What did you expect?"

He put on the wounded expression that had always gotten to her in the past. "I didn't expect you to dump six years of friendship over one little mistake."

"It wasn't the first time you lied to the media about us." And that sad look wasn't tugging at her heartstrings anymore.

Perry jerked, like he hadn't expected her to have worked that out. "It was all harmless. I needed the money. We aren't all born with the silver spoon of Archer International Holdings to feed off of."

"Telling people I was a sexual addict who couldn't be satisfied with a single partner wasn't harmless. You destroyed my reputation."

"For exactly twenty-four hours. Viktor Beck saw to that."

"Conrad is good at what he does."

"Your dad's media fixer? Yeah, I kind of expected him to get involved, but he's a cuddly kitten compared to that vicious shark you married."

"Vik protected me when *you* fed me to the wolves. I'm not sure I'd label *him* the vicious one."

"You know I didn't mean it." Perry sounded like he really expected her to believe that.

What a jerk. And this man had been one of her dearest friends for *six* years. "I knew you were lying, that's not the same thing as knowing you didn't mean it."

"I needed the money. You knew I did."

"And I refused to give it to you." Which was what it all came down to, wasn't it?

"I asked for a loan. From a *friend*."

"When have you ever paid back even a single dollar of all the money you *borrowed* from me, Perry?" she demanded, the confrontation with her ex-friend unexpectedly bringing her current situation into clear and certain focus.

Perry was that guy. The user. The manipulator. The prevaricator.

Vik was her white knight. Full stop.

He might never say the three little words she most wanted to hear, but she wasn't going to spend the rest of her life lamenting that fact. Not when he gave her so much to rejoice about instead.

"You can't guarantee business investments."

"So now they were business investments." She narrowed her eyes at Perry. "Where are my contracts showing the percentage ownership I had in those business ventures?"

"We don't need contracts between us."

She thought of the agreement Vik had forced Perry to sign. "Apparently, we do."

"Come on, Maddie. Call off your attack dog."

"Vik?"

"Who else?" Perry did his best to look beseeching.

"We aren't friends anymore and we never will be again," she spelled out very carefully.

"This is because of Romi, isn't it? She finally turned you against me."

"*You* turned me against you, Perry. You lied about me and did your best to destroy my reputation."

He'd gone back to looking wounded. "No."

"Yes. And if you'd succeeded, my dreams of starting a charter school would have been dust." At least with her name on any of the paperwork.

Perry shrugged. "San Francisco doesn't need another school."

His ability to dismiss the dreams of her heart so easily took her breath away. "I don't agree."

"Well, it didn't happen."

"No thanks to you."

"Hey, I went public with an apology and a confession that it was all a joke."

Did he expect her to thank him? "But it wasn't a joke. It was a big ugly lie. Nothing even a tiny bit amusing about that."

"Come on, Maddie. You have to forgive me."

"Yes, for my own sake. I have to let it go."

Triumph flashed in Perry's washed-out blue eyes. "We can be friends again and forget about that agreement Viktor forced me to sign."

"No."

"But—"

"No one forced you to sign anything. You signed that agreement of your own volition because you didn't want to risk being sued by both AIH and the tabloid you sold that story to."

Maddie's head snapped up at Vik's voice. What was he doing here? How had he found her?

He stood like an avenging angel over Perry. "You are not my wife's friend. She's convinced you were at one time, but that time passed long before this latest incident."

"Who do you think you are to—"

"I am the man who will *ruin* you if you come near *my* wife again." His jaw hewn from granite, Vik's eyes burned with dark fury.

Perry put his hands up. "No problem. Look, I just thought we could still be friends, but I can see you're not comfortable with that."

"I'm not comfortable with it," Maddie inserted. "Stop blaming other people for your screwup, Perry. You destroyed our friendship and Vik is right, that started a long time ago."

"But, Maddie…"

She shook her head. "No. We're over. If you see me at a function, walk the other way because I don't want to talk to you anymore."

"We aren't going to be at the same functions," he said bitterly.

Maddie didn't bother to reply. That was Perry's problem, not hers.

"Are you going to leave, or will you force me

to call the police to enforce the restraining order we have against you?"

"I'm leaving," Perry said quickly, backing out of the alcove.

"We have a restraining order?" Maddie asked Vik.

"Yes."

"Didn't I have to sign something for it?"

"No. His malicious intent was in the papers for the world to see. We filed for it on behalf of AIH and its primaries, of which you are one."

"Oh."

He looked down at her untouched coffee. "You're not drinking that."

She shook her head. "How did you find me?"

"Are you sure you want to know?"

"Yes."

"The 'find me' function on your phone."

"I turned it off."

"As long as the battery is in it and holds any charge, the GPS function works."

"So, if I want privacy, I have to take out the battery. Good to know."

He had to have looked up her GPS signal right away to have gotten to the coffee shop so quickly. More evidence that she mattered to him in the ways that were truly important.

Her father never would have just dumped his

schedule to go running after her mother, or Maddie, certainly.

Vik inhaled, opened his mouth to speak, closed it again and then said, "I would prefer you not do that."

"Okay." It was a matter of safety as well, as much as she might prefer to forget that fact. "You came after me."

"Of course. You were upset. What Jeremy did to you…"

She coughed out a laugh at the rare vulgarity that came out of her husband's mouth.

Vik put his hand out to her. "Will you come *with* me now?"

Maddie didn't hesitate. "Yes."

"Don't you want to know where?" Vik asked as she took his hand and let him lead her from the coffee shop.

"I guess I assumed we'd go someplace private."

Vik's expression turned hard. "Actually, we're going back to AIH to confront your father."

"Together."

"Yes."

Implying Vik and Maddie were on one side and Jeremy Archer the other. Nice. If she'd needed proof that she came first with Vik, her father couldn't have provided a better opportunity.

Which, okay, maybe having the proof *was* nice, but she wasn't about to thank Jeremy.

* * *

Her father was in his office when they arrived, Dr. Wilson gone. The PA tried to tell them that Jeremy was in a meeting, but Vik just walked through.

He reached across Jeremy's desk and ended the call, sending Maddie's father surging to his feet as he spluttered with annoyance.

Vik waited until her father had gone silent to speak. "Have you ever known me to lie to you?"

Jeremy shook his head, his expression instantly wary.

"Do I bluff?" Vik asked.

"No," Jeremy said shortly.

"Then you will know I mean every word I say when I tell you that if you attempt to prove Madison incompetent to forestall her giving half her shares to Romi Grayson, I will destroy Archer International Holdings until the very building we are standing in is leveled to the ground."

"You don't mean that," Jeremy said, his voice warbling with emotion for the first time in Maddie's memory.

She hadn't even seen him appear this distraught at her mother's funeral.

There was no give in Vik. Not in his expression. Not in the way he stood, towering over Jeremy's desk. "We have just established that I do."

Definitely not in his tone.

Her dad said something else, but Maddie wasn't listening. Everything inside her had gone still as she had her second major revelation for the day.

"You *do* love me," she said to Vik, ignoring her father completely.

That oh-so-serious espresso gaze fixed on her. "You are mine to protect."

"And to love." Giddy with joy that could not be tempered even by her father's machinations, she could hardly help the delight surfing every syllable.

She didn't even want to try.

Maddie beamed up at the man she'd crushed on since she was fourteen and loved since she was sixteen. "I love you, too, but you know that."

"Do you?" Vik asked. "Even now?"

"Especially now." He wasn't even remotely responsible for her father's actions.

"I meant what I said to your father." He said it like it was a warning.

"I know."

"I am utterly ruthless and without remorse."

She might argue that point, but understood that Vik believed it. And that was okay with her.

He used his powers for good, even if he didn't see it.

She smiled at him, letting her love show in her

eyes. "Your sense of honor is the shiniest and clearest facet of your nature. Everything else about you is filtered through the light it casts."

"I am not a nice guy."

"You just threatened to destroy my company," her dad said with feeling. "You sure as hell are *not* a nice guy."

Maddie's smile morphed into a full grin. "It's all a matter of perspective. I love that you would pull out every stop to slay my dragons."

"I'm not a dragon. I'm your father, damn it."

She flicked him a disgusted glance. "Who threatened to have me declared mentally incompetent."

"You can't believe I wanted things to go down that way, but you're giving away my company." Vik might claim to be remorseless, but Jeremy's expression and tone were soaked with regret.

"Don't exaggerate," she said, dismissing her father's words. "Twelve and a half percent with the voting proxy assigned to Vik and any successor he should formally appoint."

Vik jolted beside her. "I didn't know that."

"I trust you."

His gaze turned soft like she'd never expected to see. "You do."

"You knew that."

"I told myself you did."

"And me." He'd told her when she'd still been denying it to herself.

"Apparently it is different coming from you."

Her dad sighed. "You know, your mother and I never felt the need to talk our emotions to death."

Finally, Maddie gave Jeremy her attention. "Maybe if you had, things would have been different."

"I cannot change the past," he said with a pained expression.

"You spend enough time screwing up with your daughter in the present, the past is hardly what you need to be worried about," Vik told her father.

"I am sorry for ambushing you with Dr. Wilson, Madison." Jeremy looked at her with appeal. "It probably makes no difference to you, but I told Dr. Wilson I wouldn't be needing his services immediately after you left my office."

"That's hard to believe." Her father didn't back down once he'd set a course of action in motion.

He just didn't. And he *did* lie.

Jeremy said, "Call him. He'll tell you."

Bluffing or truth?

"He's telling the truth," Vik told her.

Maddie looked up at her husband. "How can you tell?"

"His eyes shift to the left when he's lying about something important."

"And this is important to him?" she asked with suspicion.

"It involves you and his company. There is nothing more important to him."

That she believed. At least the part about the company.

"Why did you tell Dr. Wilson to back off?" she asked.

Jeremy shifted uncomfortably in his chair. "I knew that if I followed through with my plan, you would never forgive me."

"Are you sure it wasn't because you realized that my marriage to Vik would be invalidated if I was deemed unfit to make legal decisions?"

Her father's eyes widened, his skin going pale. A reaction he could not fake. He *hadn't* thought of that. "No wonder Vik pulled out the rocket launchers."

"He wants to be married to me more than he wants to be president of AIH." Just saying the words gave her emotional satisfaction to the very depths of her being.

Jeremy nodded, his expression more vulnerable than she'd ever seen it. "I hope you've worked out that I want to be your dad more than I want control of those shares."

It was her turn to nod, but maybe with not as much conviction.

"It might benefit you both if your father attended some sessions with you and Dr. MacKenzie," Vik said.

Maddie waited to see her father's reaction to that piece of advice before offering her own.

Jeremy Archer shocked her to the very marrow of his bones when he said, "I would like that very much. Are you willing, Madison?"

"I don't know." What if he used the time they had together with the therapist to compile ammunition against her?

"Do you believe Vik will destroy Archer International Holdings if I attempt to have you declared mentally incompetent?"

"Yes." There was not a single atom in her body that did not trust Vik to do just that.

"Then you have nothing to fear," her father said, showing he'd guessed correctly what had her hesitating.

"I'll talk to Dr. MacKenzie. If she thinks it's a good idea, we'll arrange the sessions."

Her dad startled her again, getting up from his desk and coming around to kiss her on the cheek and shake Vik's hand. "Thank you for watching out for her better than I ever have."

"I always will." It was another Viktor Beck promise.

And the places still cold inside from Maddie's unexpected meetings with her father, the psychiatrist and then Perry, warmed. "And I will watch out for Vik."

Starting with taking him home and teaching him how to say three all-important words.

"I believe you. You have your mother's loyalty and my stubbornness. He couldn't be in better hands."

Maddie surprised herself, accepting the compliment with the warmth it was intended. "Thank you."

Vik slid his arm around her waist. "It's time for us to go home, I think."

"What about your afternoon meetings?" she asked, not really wanting him to go back to work.

But now that she knew he loved her, Maddie could wait for the evening to hear him say it. Maybe.

"I canceled everything after your phone call."

"Because nothing is more important to you than I am," she said with satisfaction.

Vik could have shrugged. He could have tried to deny it. He could have grimaced in unhappy acknowledgment.

He did none of those things.

What he did was turn his big body to face her, blocking out her view of her dad and his office.

Vik cupped Maddie's cheeks, his hands trembling against her skin. "Exactly."

Oh, man. She was going to melt right there.

"Take me home, please," she said, her voice low with fervency.

Vik made a sound like something had broken inside him and then leaned down and kissed her. His mouth claimed hers with undeniable need. She gave in to it without hesitation.

Maddie didn't know how long the kiss lasted, but when her father's voice finally penetrated, she was pressed against Vik, his arms tight bands around her.

"Sheesh, you two need to go home."

"Kicking us out?" Vik asked with no evidence of embarrassment at what they were doing.

Her dad, on the other hand, had a definite ruddy cast to his cheeks. "What's coming next is not going to happen in my office."

Maddie's own cheeks heated at the implication of his words. He was absolutely right. It was time to leave.

The trip home happened in a haze for her and Maddie was glad Vik drove.

He surprised her by pulling her into the morning room, the shabby chic so like her former apartment and cheery lemon-yellow accents barely registering as he pulled her to sit with him on the deep sofa.

"I thought we were going upstairs." To make love.

That's certainly where their kiss in her father's office had been leading.

"We're going to talk." Vik winced as if the words pained him. "About the emotional stuff."

"Can't we do that later?" Knowing he loved her was making her desire for the physical proof overwhelming.

"No."

"Why not?" She wasn't whining.

She wasn't, but so far, her day had sort of sucked. Making love with her husband? Now, after learning he was in love with her, that would take this one into the "best days ever" category.

"Because maybe things would have been different for Helene and Jeremy if they had," Vik said, quoting her own words back at her.

"That was them. We aren't my parents."

"No, we aren't." Vik took a deep breath and let it out, his complexion just a little green. "I love you, Madison."

She didn't tease him for nearly being sick with stress over the admission, though the temptation was great. But she appreciated how hard this had to be for her usually single-minded, alpha business tycoon.

"Maddie."

"What?" he asked, like she'd strayed from the script.

"You love me. I love you. You call me Maddie, like Romi does."

"Perry, too." And Vik didn't appear happy about that.

"Not anymore. Perry doesn't get to call me anything. You saw to that."

"The restraining order lasts two years, but we'll renew it."

She shook her head. "I don't need the restraining order. Trust me, you're enough, Vik."

"He approached you."

"So, I'll stop going to that coffee shop."

"That won't be necessary. I'll buy it and have him banned."

"Can you say overkill here, Vik?"

"Nothing is too much to protect you."

"Oh, man." She saw a lifetime ahead of her of reining in Vik's impulses to keep even the hint of harm from her and the children they would have.

Honestly? The image had a pretty rosy glow.

"Do you want me to leave AIH?" he asked.

"What? No!" It was her turn to reach out and cup his face, meeting his eyes with an expression as sincere as she could make it. "I do not need you to give up your dreams to believe you love me."

Though knowing he was willing to heal wounds in her heart from twenty-four years as Jeremy Archer's daughter.

"I do. I did six years ago, but…"

"You didn't recognize what the feeling was," she guessed.

"No. I'd never been in love."

"I'm glad." The thought she could have lost him before she ever had the chance to catch his eye sent cold tremors through her.

"I didn't think I needed love."

"We all need love."

Vik frowned. "I'm not sure that is true."

He sounded so uncertain, so very unlike the man she was used to. But this was not his area of expertise.

Emotions were almost as foreign to Vik as they were to her dad.

"It's okay, Vik. We love each other and we are going to be very happy."

"Aren't we happy right now?"

Giving in to the urge, she threw herself into his arms with a laugh. "Yes, my darling, wonderful husband. We are very happy."

He caught her to him, responding to her kiss and holding her tight.

Oh, yes, *very* happy.

They made love, right there on the sofa, and practiced saying those three little words to each other.

EPILOGUE

Vᴵᴋ ᴀɢʀᴇᴇᴅ ᴡɪᴛʜ Maddie and Romi on the property they picked out for the charter school. Declaring it the perfect location, he insisted on putting an offer in on it immediately.

Afterward, he took her and Romi out for champagne to celebrate.

"Isn't this a bit premature?" Romi asked as they clinked glasses. "The offer hasn't been accepted yet."

Maddie just laughed. "The sellers could be a business consortium of questionable pedigree and they wouldn't have a chance against Vik."

"We'll get the property," Vik said as if there simply wasn't another option.

Maddie was pretty sure with her tycoon on the case, there wasn't.

Romi grinned, lifting her glass toward Vik. "To business shark negotiators and dreams coming true."

They didn't go straight home after, but Vik took Maddie back up to the overlook at Marin

Headlands. She didn't ask what they were doing there.

Maddie just held his hand as they traversed the path to what many considered the best place for viewing San Francisco's skyline.

He stopped in the same spot he'd proposed. "We forgot some promises when we were here before."

"Did we?"

He nodded. "You forgot to promise not to leave your security detail behind anymore."

That wasn't what she was expecting him to say, but it was so in line with Vik and his priorities that she grinned. "Duly noted."

"Promise."

She put her hand over her heart. "I promise to keep my security detail with me."

"Your days of volunteering anonymously are over." He leaned down and kissed her. "I'm sorry."

"It's okay. You'll just have to find me a detail that likes children."

"I think that can be arranged."

Suddenly she realized why they were dealing with this now. "If my detail had been with me when I went to the coffee shop, Perry wouldn't have gotten within ten feet of me."

"If that."

"Right."

Vik shrugged. "Do you think Romi would allow me to assign a detail to her as well?"

"What? Why?"

"She is your sister-by-choice."

"I didn't know you were aware of that."

"Your mother considered her another daughter."

"She did." Maddie smiled in memory. "But I'm not sure Romi needs security because I consider her my sister."

"In a few weeks, she will own twelve and a half percent of a multibillion-dollar company."

"No one but us will know that."

"You know better than that."

She did. "I don't know if we can convince her."

"Tell her security comes with the shares."

"She's not going to be happy."

Vik didn't look too worried about that reality. "She's part of my family now. She'll get used to it."

Maddie wasn't sure she agreed, but she loved the sentiment.

Vik pulled Maddie close, but kept eye contact. "I love you."

It didn't matter that he'd said it before, that she knew it to be true—saying the words here made them a vow for him.

Maddie's throat constricted, moisture burning hot behind her eyes and all she could do was nod.

"I will love you always," he promised.

She took a steadying breath. "Me, too."

"We *will* say the important stuff."

"Yes."

"We'll talk about the emotional stuff often." He still looked a little green around the gills at the idea, but he was making the promise.

And Maddie knew Vik would keep it.

"With our children, too," Maddie vowed.

Vik nodded. "When I forget, you'll remind me."

"Yes." Not that she was convinced he would ever forget the important things.

When Vik set his mind to something, he succeeded.

He looked like he had something he wanted to say, so she waited for him to say it. "Your father…"

"Yes?"

"I could have been him."

"No. You're different."

"I am, but I could have been. He never got that love and family made having the power and the business matter, not the other way around."

"But you do."

"I do." The absolute conviction in Vik's tone touched her to the core.

"Perry really played into your hands, didn't he?"

Vik shrugged. "We would have married, one way, or another."

"Because you loved me and could not imagine your life without me."

Vik's smile was brighter than the sun in the height of summer. "Exactly."

"Ditto."

Their shared laughter floated over the bay as their bodies pressed together in the most basic promise of all.

Shared love for a lifetime.

* * * * *

If you enjoyed this book,
look out for Max and Romi's story in
A VIRGIN FOR HIS PRIZE
by Lucy Monroe.
Coming soon!